I0603067

break
AWAY
SAFFRON BLU

Editing: Tiny Tiger Edits

Formatting: Saffron Blu

Cover Design: Cover Me Darling LLC

BLURB

Mitch Sewell's boxing career was just taking off when the unimaginable happened.

He killed someone in the ring.

Vowing never to step foot in a boxing ring again, he retires to run the gym he part owns and teach self-defence classes.

Every day is a constant battle against the memories crippling him.

That is until the day someone walks through the gym door and gives him a brief glance of how different his life could be, if only he can overcome his baggage.

Can Mitch break away from the guilt, or will it keep him chained forever?

DEAR READER

Please note that parts of Break Away was released as a short story in the Love is Love: An LGBTQI Charity Anthology, since receiving her rights back Saffron has added extra content to double the original stories length and make it a novella.

Saffron Blu is Australian so there will be Aussie-isms in this book.

This book has been written using UK English and is set in Australia, with Australian characters.

I apologise if there are words or phrases you don't understand. Please feel free to contact Saffron for further explanation, or to discuss the meaning of a particular phrase or word, via her website or any of her social media accounts.

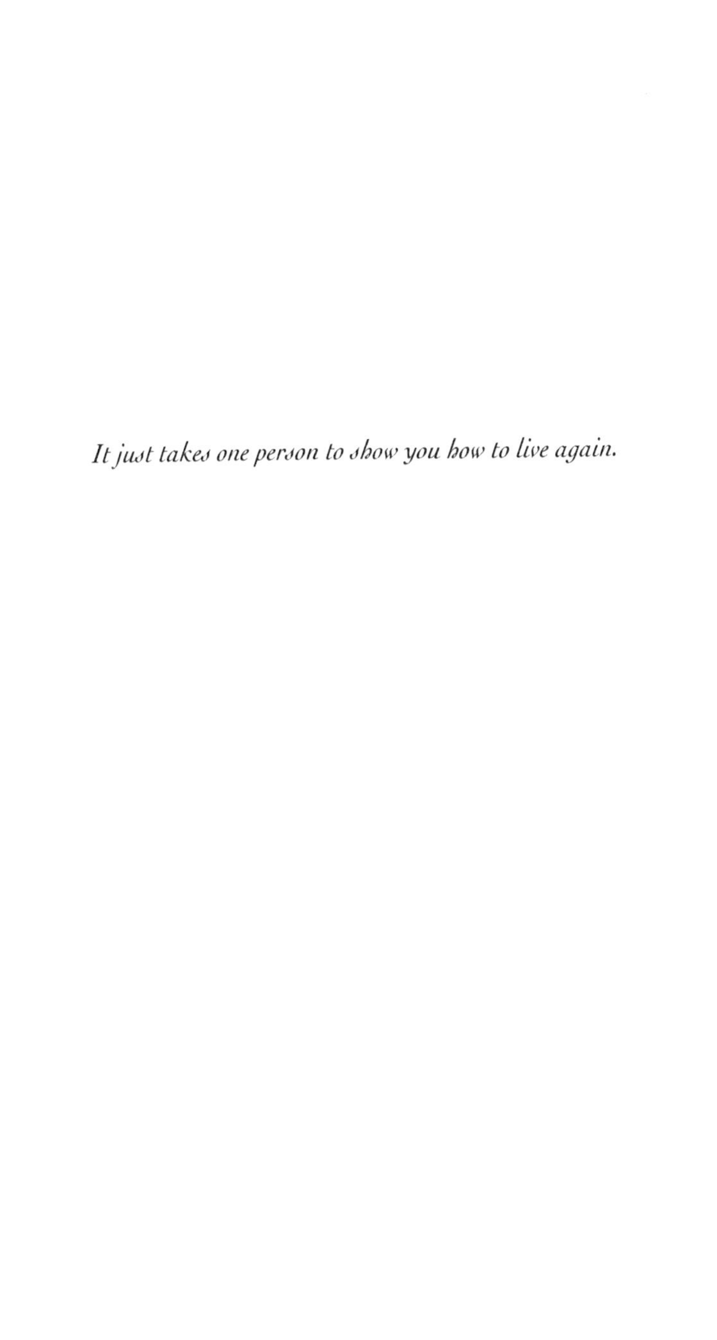

It just takes one person to show you how to live again.

PROLOGUE

MITCH

THIS WAS IT.

The fight of Mitch's career. He glanced over the shoulder of his opponent, the undefeated champion, Boone Carter, and caught sight of his trainer and best friend, Joey, who gave him a short nod from between the ropes. Mitch knew exactly what he'd meant by that.

It was time to stop playing.

It was time to end the fight.

They were in the tenth round and they'd both managed to land some good hits so it was too close to call who would win.

Mitch needed to land a knockout punch before the bout ended.

Boone's glove connected with Mitch's jaw and his vision blurred. He stumbled back into the ropes and shook his head, hoping to clear his sight, before blindly throwing out a left hook.

Boone went down like a sack of potatoes.

The referee crouched beside Boone and instantly felt for a pulse as everyone watched on, waiting to see some movement from the reigning champ. Mitch was close enough to see the referee's face drain of all colour seconds before he turned Boone on his back and started CPR.

Boone's trainer and another man shoved past Mitch and dropped beside the referee, shouting for Boone to wake up.

Mitch's mind spun as he stared down at his shaking fists. Strong hands pulled at his shoulders, directing him towards the changing rooms, the sound of the chaos in the ring disappearing with every step they took.

ONE

MITCH - ONE YEAR LATER

MITCH COUNTED the gloves on the floor to make sure he had enough for the students that were signed up to his new self-defence course and, once satisfied, he headed to reception so he could greet the students of his first session as they arrived.

He found Joey, his business partner, ex-trainer, and best friend, rummaging through the drawers behind the desk.

"Joey, it took me all morning to organise that fuck-ton of paperwork, don't you dare mess that shit up," Mitch warned.

Joey turned his chocolate brown eyes on Mitch. "Organise? You call this organised? I can't find fuck all anymore."

"It's much better than your organised chaos." Mitch rolled his eyes. "What is it you're looking for anyway?"

His friend started rifling through the papers in the top drawer. "There was a scrap of paper that had a number on it. It was tucked under the mouse pad, but it's not there now."

Mitch grinned, knowing exactly why Joey was panicking about not finding the number. Rose was a pretty little thing and Joey had been trying to organise a date for months. Last week on her way out of training she finally caved and gave him her number. Mitch was sure she only did it to shut him up, but it looked like after a week of sitting on it Joey was ready to make the call.

Mitch swiped at the iPad on the desk and, after bringing up the relevant contact, he turned the screen so Joey could see it.

Joey stared at the screen.

Mitch expected to see a smile but his face looked even more sour. "What?" When Joey didn't reply he carried on. "She's a member, we already had her number on file."

"But she gave me her number."

"And? You've got permission to use it for something other than gym business." Mitch couldn't see what Joey was getting all worked up for. Had he wanted to keep the piece of paper as a memento or something?

Joey sighed and pulled out his phone, entering the digits before holding it up to his ear. Without a glance in Mitch's direction he quickly slipped through the door that led towards the staff room, obviously looking for privacy. Not that he'd get any in there. As soon as the other staff members caught on to what the call was about they'd be heckling him to no end.

The bell above the door rang and Mitch turned, all thoughts of Joey and Rose leaving his head as his eyes fell on the cute wiry guy that stopped in front of the desk with a wary look on his face.

Green eyes slowly worked their way up his torso, pausing on his pecs that could be seen through the loose fitted singlet he was wearing.

Mitch cleared his throat and wide green orbs darted to meet his.

"Hi…Erm…I'm…Shit." He rubbed a hand over his face and Mitch suddenly felt sorry for the guy.

"Shit? That's an unusual name. Nice to meet you Shit, I'm Mitch," he said, a wide grin spreading across his face.

That sage green gaze once again met his and Mitch was relieved to see the earlier worry and embarrassment had been replaced with amusement. "While 'Shit' would make a pretty cool name, that's unfortunately not what my mother named me." He offered his hand to shake. "I'm Lore. Nice to meet you, Mitch."

Mitch took his hand and noted how firm his shake was, despite his callus free fingers and palms letting him know the man in front of him didn't do a lot of manual labour. Taking in Lore's frame, that didn't surprise him. "Nice to meet you, Lore. Are you here for the self-defence class?"

The other man swallowed nervously as they ended their handshake. "Yeah. I bet your classes are usually full of women."

Mitch shook his head and brought up the list of students that were meant to be coming today on his iPad. "Not at all. It's the first class today and there seems to be an almost even number of guys and girls. See?" He turned the screen so Lore could easily read it.

Lore's shoulders sagged in relief. "That's good to know."

Mitch ran through the list looking for Lore's name so he could mark him off as attending. "I can't seem to find Lore on here. Did you pre-book or were you hoping to just jump in?" he asked.

"I'm booked in by my full name, Lorcan Cole," he admitted with a grimace. The guy clearly wasn't a fan of his name, but Mitch kinda liked it, having always been a fan of the less popular names.

Mitch ticked him off and flicked through the security cards that had been set up for the new students. "Okay, Lore. This is your security card. It will get you into the locker room and you can use it to access a locker once you're in there." Lore bit his lip, clearly concerned about something, and Mitch went on hoping to ease the guy's worries. "There are signs everywhere and the steps are pretty simple. The gym is open twenty-four-seven so you can work out anytime. Your card unlocks the main door when it's out of regular business hours and there are no staff members around. It also automatically takes care of the lights on entry and exit too. The swiping device is just to the right of the door."

Lore nodded. "I spotted that as I came in. I don't think I'll be using the gym other than when you have the classes on. I'm not really a gym person."

"It's part of your package so I've got to tell you about it, just in case."

The bell above the door rang, drawing his attention to the group of three chatting girls who were stepping in.

He quickly turned back to Lore, not wanting a big queue to form. "If you want to head through to the men's locker room, you can get changed and store your things in a locker. Class will start in the main dojo in about ten minutes. It's clearly sign-posted so you shouldn't get lost."

Lore raised his brows. "I'm pretty good at get-ting lost, so we'll have to see about that."

Mitch's eyes followed Lore as he scanned his card and headed through the locker room door. He hadn't allowed himself to be interested in anyone since his last fight—Joey seemed to think he was punishing himself but Mitch was sure it was just that he hadn't been attracted to anyone—yet he now found himself wondering what was so dif-ferent about Lore since he was definitely catching his attention.

TWO

LORE

LORE OBSERVED Mitch as he took a long swig of his water bottle. Mitch's dark hair was sticking up in all directions due to the hand he'd been running through it during the lesson and Lore couldn't help but find it appealing. He usually went for the well-presented guys. *You know, the ones who are preened to perfection, not a hair out of place.* It flitted through his mind that maybe that was why his relationships never lasted. The guys he usually picked were all too into themselves to even see him, let alone love him.

While some of the students around the dojo chatted amongst themselves, and others discreetly exited, Lore decided to take things out of his comfort zone and try to start a conversation with Mitch. He'd always been socially awkward but when it came to guys he liked, things just got worse.

"Thanks, Mitch," Lore said, his heart beating erratically in his chest.

Mitch turned, his brown eyes locking onto Lore's. "Will we see you again next week?"

"Most definitely, I really enjoyed it tonight," he admitted with a nod.

"You did real well. You're a quick study." Mitch winked and Lore's stomach flipped with nerves at the sight. *Was Mitch flirting or was he just being friendly?* He'd picked him out a number of times in the lesson to demonstrate moves and at the time Lore could only worry about how idiotic he'd look as he failed but now he wondered if that too was Mitch's way of flirting.

Lore felt his cheeks heat with embarrassment but pride at the compliment soon took precedence. "I had a good teacher," he said before he averted his gaze, a fresh wave of embarrassment falling over him with the admission.

He was used to being a bit of a social pariah but his undeniable attraction to the Hot God before him seemed to double his affliction.

A couple of girls stepped up. "There are a few of us going to go get a drink at the tavern, do you guys fancy joining us?" She waved her arm in the direction of a mixed group of people milling around the doorway, clearly waiting for them.

Lore lifted his eyes to Mitch, wanting to hear his answer before he replied with his own.

Mitch's frown gave away his answer before he even opened his mouth. "Sadly, I can't make it. I offered to take Mikayla's spin class, which starts in ten minutes. You guys have fun though." He ran a hand through his hair and Lore's hand itched to reach out and see if Mitch's dark strands were as soft as they looked.

Fisting his hand at his side, he reminded himself it was creepy to touch a guy like that when you'd only just met them.

"How about you? It's Lore, right?"

Lore's eyes darted to the girl who'd just said his name. "Me?" he said, surprise clear in his higher than normal pitched voice. People rarely invited him places and they never remembered his name.

She gave him a sure smile and a nod.

"Erm…well, I don't know. I…" He stumbled over his words as he decided what to do. He didn't have many friends and knew, deep down, that he needed to step out of his comfort zone and find a group of people he could call his own. He was much too old to be sharing his older brother's mates. And with that thought fresh in his mind he jumped in with both feet. "Sure. I'd love to."

"That's fantastic!" The girl sounded genuinely excited at the prospect as she grabbed Lore's hand and tugged him towards the others by the door.

Lore's eyes flitted between Mitch and the back of the girl's head as he could do nothing but follow behind her.

Mitch lifted a hand in a wave. "See you next week."

Lore knew the gesture was for everyone, but his crazy mind was already obsessing over the handsome trainer and he couldn't help but imagine it was just for him.

"Mitch'll meet you there after the spin class. I'll make sure of it." A blond guy in a loose singlet with the gym's logo on it and shorts announced with a wink as they passed him in the doorway.

Lore's heart hammered erratically in his chest knowing he'd see Mitch again…and soon.

WITHIN FIFTEEN MINUTES they were all seated in the tavern across the road from the gym. They'd pushed a couple of tables together and the other two guys—Brad and Gazza—headed to the bar to buy the first round.

Lore turned his attention to Stacy; the girl who'd invited him out in the first place and seemed to have taken him under her wing, choosing to start a conversation with him the minute she'd sat down. He brushed his hair back as he felt it fall over his forehead and suddenly regretted showering at the gym without having any wax or gel on hand to keep his hair tamed.

"Listen to me prattling on about myself," Stacy stated with a shake of her head, clearly annoyed at herself. "Tell us about you, Lore. What brought you to the self-defence classes?"

Lore glanced between the three girls sat at the table wondering whether he could come out and tell them such a personal thing. They were virtually strangers after all.

Stacy's piercing blue eyes locked onto his and she gave him a gentle smile. "I could prattle on more if you'd like?"

Lore chuckled.

Rebecca, a pretty brunette leant forward with a hand on her heart. "Oh god no, please save us from having to suffer that."

Stacy huffed playfully. "Becca, you're so mean. You're meant to be my best friend."

"You know I love you really," Becca said as she gave Stacy a sweet smile.

"Becca and I could tell you our stories first, if that will make it easier for you?" the third and final girl of the group, Natasha, offered.

Lore shook his head. "No, it's fine, honest. I was mugged a couple of weeks ago and it made me feel weak. I felt like I had to do something so that I could fight back if it happened again."

Stacy nodded in agreement. "That's how I felt about Brian," she admitted, mentioning the ex who, as she'd just told them, beat her on a regular basis. "I didn't want another guy to be able overpower me again and the only way I can control that is by learning how to defend myself."

"You're so brave, Stacy." Natasha stared at Stacy with admiration clear in her gaze.

A clunking sound drew everyone's attention to Brad who placed two jugs of lager on the table before pushing them in to the middle. "Have no fear, the drink is finally here. Gazza's got the glasses." He stated, hooking a finger over his shoulder in the direction of the guy following him.

Lore's eyes fell on the tall chestnut-haired guy approaching the table carrying a tray. As he bent to place it on the table Lore spotted the six shot glasses full of black liquid which had been out of sight behind the empty frosted glasses.

"Right guys, grab a shot, we're making a toast," Gazza said as he lifted his own shot glass off the tray.

Stacy, Rebecca, and Brad all followed suit as Natasha looked at the remaining glasses nervously.

Lore sympathised with Natasha. He wasn't a big drinker and knew if he threw back one of those shots he'd be a drunken mess in no time but, even knowing that, he grabbed one of the remaining glasses. He wanted to make friends and thought if he lowered his inhibitions just a little, he'd be relaxed enough to do that.

Natasha sighed but swiped up the lone glass on the tray. "What are we toasting to?"

"Becoming bad arses," Gazza stated.

"And new friends," Stacy added.

With a round of agreement they all clinked glasses and knocked back their shots.

Lore shuddered as the fiery liquid flowed down his throat.

"What the fuck was that? It was god awful." Rebecca winced as she poured herself a glass of lager before guzzling a good mouthful down.

Gazza laughed. "Black Sambuca."

Rebecca screwed up her face. "It tasted like…"

"Liquorice," Lore offered, before admitting, "I kinda liked it."

"Yes, that's it. I hate liquorice." Becca shuddered as she had another smaller sip of her beer.

Brad poured everyone a glass of lager and Gazza took the tray with empty shot glasses back to the bar before taking the seat next to Natasha, Brad sitting at the head of the table.

"How long have you all known each other?" Lore blurted out, even surprising himself.

Everyone seemed to lock eyes before anyone

spoke, as if they were silently deciding who should answer.

It was Stacy who spoke up first. "Me and Becca have known each other since we were in nappies."

"I work with Becca and Brad," Natasha offered. "I've met Stacy a couple of times through Becca.

"And I'm Brad's roommate. I only met the girls tonight," Gazza informed Lore.

Stacy sat forward in her seat as she looked at him with eager eyes. "What's going on between you and Mitch?"

Lore frowned. "Nothing. I only met him tonight."

The girls gave each other a look that Lore couldn't quite decipher.

"The chemistry between you two...I could have sworn..." Stacy shook her head in dismissal.

"Mitch is gay?" Gazza asked, disbelief in his voice.

Lore eyed Gazza for a minute trying to work out where his question was heading. Could Gazza be homophobic? This friendship wouldn't work out if that were the case, for obvious reasons. Lore wasn't in the closet. Never had been.

"Do you have a problem if he is?" Lore glanced around the table with wide eyes as he realised it was him who'd asked that question.

Gazza recoiled. "What? Fuck, no. I don't have a problem with you being gay. I just didn't think Mitch was, he doesn't seem the type...Fuck. I sound like a total dick." He shook his head, clearly pissed with himself. "I'm gonna buy another round of shots in apology." Scooting his chair back without another word he shoved his hands in his pockets and strode towards the bar.

"He really isn't a homophobe, I promise," Brad announced as he watched his mate at the bar.

Lore knew that was the truth. If Gazza's actions didn't show it, the sincerity in Brad's voice did. That wasn't what was bothering Lore at that moment, it was what Gazza had said. *'You being gay'.* Everyone seemed to *know* Lore was gay before he even made it clear and it wasn't like he was overly effeminate or anything. Lore knew it wasn't worth questioning because no one could ever explain how they *just knew.*

He waved Brad off. "I get it. It's all good."

Gazza came back to the table with another round of shots. "Bottoms up guys and gals." He held his glass out waiting for the others to grab theirs and clink their glasses. They all did just that.

"Love is love," Lore toasted, only worrying a little that he'd maybe chosen the wrong thing to say, before the others eagerly joined him in his toast with a chorus of *'love is love'.* Lore's heart was suddenly lighter as he swallowed down what was fast becoming his favourite drink.

THREE

MITCH

As Mitch gave his bike seat a quick wipe down he looked up to find one last client grabbing her bottle from the floor. "See ya, Mitch," she called out.

Mitch waved her off and couldn't help but be glad his classes for the day were over. It didn't mean he could go home yet; he still had a heap of admin work to do before that could happen, but at least he didn't have to interact with people.

As he made his way through the gym, he counted a couple of guys still working out and another two sparring in the ring.

Mitch missed boxing and the exhilaration it gave him as he just let go in the ring, but that wasn't him anymore. No matter how much he longed for it, he'd never step into a ring again. Shoving all thoughts of boxing away he focused back on where he was heading.

As Mitch stepped into the small box of an office

off the reception area, Joey looked up from the desk.

"Hey."

Mitch frowned as he checked his watch. "Joey, what are you doing here? You're usually home by now."

He gestured to the papers in front of him. "These forms aren't going to enter themselves."

"I always do that before I go home, that's why I'm here now. You head off," Mitch stated, feeling somewhat insulted that Joey seemed to think he wasn't doing his job well enough.

Joey focused back on the screen before him, clicking away at the keyboard. "You're going to meet the others at the tavern."

Mitch's eyes widened. "I'm *what* now?" he said, his voice coming out higher than normal.

Joey sighed and stood up, moving from behind the desk to lean against the front corner. "Mitch, you've been punishing yourself for long enough. It's been a year. You need to get over it."

"Over it? Boone died." Mitch couldn't hold back the anger in his voice as he fisted his hands by his hips.

"It was an accident. You've read the medical report." Joey lifted his hands in defence and carried on before Mitch could react to his words. "I know you won't get in the ring again and, as much as that's a fucking big shame and waste of talent, no one can force you. But I'll be damned if I let you waste your life hiding in this gym. So, you're going to the tavern and you're going to have a couple of drinks with those nice people. Especially that guy you took a shine to."

Mitch's cheeks heated at the thought that his attraction had been so obvious and he dropped his eyes to the floor as he wondered whether he should bother trying to deny it.

"Don't even think about trying to come up with some lame arse excuse. You're going and that's final. I'll walk you across if I have to," Joey added, and Mitch rolled his eyes.

"That won't be necessary." Mitch sighed, knowing Joey was right and he'd follow through on that threat if he had to. "What about your mum?" Joey's mum was a stickler for routine, and he was certain she wouldn't like the fact that Joey was running late today.

"I called her earlier, she was more than happy that you'd be getting out. You know how much she thinks of you as another son." The grin on Joey's face made it clear he knew he'd won.

Mitch and Joey had grown up together, trained together and, when Mitch started showing some real skill, Joey stepped back and decided to help train Mitch. They spent most of their days during the summer holidays in Joey's garage. His house was like his second home, and Martina another mum; he loved her as such and he'd do everything he could to keep her happy.

"Fine, but if they've left already I'm coming back here and you're going home," Mitch ordered, happy to feel a little control returning to him with his demanding tone.

Joey grinned like the cat that got the cream. "Well, you better get a quick shower and get over there then."

Mitch huffed and headed for the showers in silence, his mind running, already stressing over what he was going to say when he got to the tavern. *What if they thought he was gate crashing?*

WITH A FINAL DEEP breath Mitch pushed open the doors to the tavern, his eyes instantly falling on the group he'd been teaching self-defence only just over an hour earlier. They were hard to miss, being the rowdiest bunch in the room; they clearly hadn't wasted time since arriving.

Stacy and Rebecca were dancing beside the table to what Mitch recognised as a Beyoncé song. Stacy tugged on Lore's hand obviously trying to get him to join them. He shook his head but Stacy didn't let up and Lore suddenly stood having no other option.

"Mitch!" Brad called out and all eyes in the room landed on him. Thankfully there were only a handful of people scattered throughout the rest of the tavern and none of them seemed to be as inebriated as his group of…*students*…*clients*…*friends*… He didn't even know what to think of them as.

Mitch had never been out for drinks with his clients before and wouldn't have tonight if Joey hadn't stood in the car park watching him until he entered the damn building. He knew if he hadn't, Joey would have marched him over himself. He'd made that perfectly clear when he offered to *show him the way.*

"Hey," Mitch greeted the group with a wave, feeling lame.

"*Mitch!*" Stacy squealed as she all but threw

herself at him, whist dragging Lore along with her still having a tight hold on his hand. "Your friend said you'd come but I didn't know if he was serious."

"He was so serious he watched me walk in," Mitch stated with a laugh, hoping to sound like he was at ease with it all.

Mitch glanced at Lore, who was blatantly checking him out. He gave him a lazy once-over, hovering over his groin for far longer than publicly appropriate while he bit at his lip.

Mitch grinned as Lore's eyes finally reached his own and a bright blush coloured his cheeks.

Lore cleared his throat as he flitted his gaze around the tavern to avoid Mitch's, obviously embarrassed at being caught ogling. "Shots! We need more shots," he shouted as he spun on his heel and headed for the bar, looking pretty unsteady on his feet.

"Good man! I'll come help," a ginger-haired guy who Mitch remembered to be called Gary stated.

"Ugh…not more of that black shit," Rebecca said, her face screwed up in disgust.

Mitch was thankful that he'd been the one to sign everyone in this afternoon, because that meant he at least remembered all their names.

Stacy pulled out a chair and gestured towards it. "Mitch, sit here."

"Gazza, get another glass for Mitch," Brad called across the room and Gary gave him a thumbs up as he leant towards the bartender, most probably asking for the glass.

Within seconds Lore and Gazza were back with a tray lined with shots. "Time for another toast,"

Gazza said as he placed an empty chilled glass in front of Mitch. "Help yourself to the jugs. One's lager and the other cider." He stared at them both for a second like he was trying to decipher which was which before shrugging it off. "I'm sure you'll figure it out."

Mitch laughed as he took a shot glass that was held out towards him. These guys were clearly having a party.

"Okay. What are we toasting this time?" Rebecca asked as everyone raised their mini-glasses ready to toast.

"New friends," Lore offered, his eyes locked onto Mitch's.

"And love interests," Stacy blurted.

Worry filled Lore's eyes and he pinned Stacy with a look Mitch couldn't quite interpret.

Stacy gave him a grin and clinked her glass before throwing back her shot.

Everyone followed her lead and downed theirs too.

Everyone except Rebecca, who passed hers off to Lore. "Here, have mine. I can't face another one of those."

Mitch watched Lore sway as he poured back the hard liquor and couldn't help but wonder if maybe Rebecca wasn't the only one who shouldn't be having another drink.

Lore dropped into the seat beside Mitch and turned to face him, his eyes struggling to focus on him as he spoke. "How was bike class?"

"Bike class?" Mitch's lip twitched. "Bike class was okay," he admitted, unable to hold back his chuckle.

"You've got a pretty mouth."

Mitch couldn't stop from licking his lips at Lore's drunken admission.

The girls burst into laughter and Lore tore his eyes away to look in their direction, a look of shock on his face, before he covered his eyes with his hands as he let out a groan. "I said that out loud, didn't I?"

"Afraid so, lover boy." Becca patted him on the head in sympathy.

It wasn't long before Gazza drew everyone's attention to him by saying something outrageous. Not that Mitch paid any attention. He was focused on Lore, who was still hiding his head in his hands.

"So, Mitch, how come you don't box anymore?"

Those words of Gazza's were what finally caught his attention. His eyes instantly fell on Gazza. "I…" He didn't know how to answer that. It wasn't like he was surprised to be asked the question. It had been all over the news when it had happened. Even people who didn't follow boxing would have heard about it. It was just that he hadn't explained his reasoning to anyone. Not even his best mate, Joey. Although, Mitch was more than aware that Joey knew it all even if he'd never said it aloud.

"Gazza." Stacy slapped at his arm. "You can't ask things like that. He hardly knows us." Her eyes fell on Mitch's. "Seriously Mitch, ignore him."

She grabbed Gazza and pulled him out of his seat. "Come on, we're gonna dance."

After an hour of drinking and dancing Mitch was ready to call it a night. Granted, he'd barely had more than a glass of beer and that first shot but

having seen how drunk everyone else was he figured someone needed to stay reasonably sober.

"I'm beat!" Stacy announced as she dropped
into the seat beside Mitch.

"I was just thinking about calling it a night."
Mitch lifted his warm beer to his lips.

She eyed him, warily. "Don't think I haven't noticed that you've hardly touched that since you
arrived."

Shoving the glass aside, Mitch turned to look at
Stacy. "You're pretty observant."

"That I am." She grinned. "Do you want to
know what else I've observed tonight?" Her eyes
flicked to Lore who was dancing with Becca and
Natasha a few feet away.

Mitch's eyes followed, he couldn't help it. He'd
hardly taken his eyes off Lore all night. Watching
his hips sway to the music made him wish he could
step up to join him.

"You want Lore."

Mitch didn't bother denying it because, quite
frankly, he wasn't surprised Stacy had picked up on
it. After all he hadn't been merely stealing glances,
he'd been downright staring.

Before he could reply, the subject of the conversation came stumbling towards them and caught
himself with his hands on the table.

"Hey! I think…" Lore swallowed. "I'm gonna
be—" He was cut off by a stream of vomit.

On reflex, Mitch shoved one of the almost
empty beer jugs in the line of fire to save the bar-
tenders needing to clean up the mess.

Stacy placed a hand over her mouth. "Oh god."

"Stace. Walk away," Becca ordered as she took

quick strides towards them. "She's a sympathetic spewer, we seriously don't need her joining in."

She rubbed a hand over Lore's back soothingly as Stacy quickly disappeared in the direction of the ladies' room. "Let it out, handsome."

Lore lifted his head from the jug enough to be heard but didn't make eye contact with anyone. "I think I'm okay now."

"Here." Natasha appeared, offering a handful of napkins to Lore before swapping the jug for an empty one she'd brought.

Pulling out the nearest chair, Lore sat down and hung his head over the clean jug with a groan. "I'm gonna sit…just for a minute."

Giving Lore one last pat on the back Rebecca lifted her eyes to Mitch's. "Are you alright here? I'm gonna go get rid of this." She gestured towards the vomit-filled jug. "Then I best check on Stacy."

Mitch gave her a nod. "I'll stay with Lore."

Natasha followed Rebecca without a word and Mitch caught sight of Brad and Gazza heading in his and Lore's direction.

Brad rubbed a hand over the back of his head as he glanced towards the toilets. "Our Uber's here, can you say bye to the girls for us? And let Becca and Tash know I'll see them at work on Monday?"

Mitch nodded. "No problem, catch you at next week's class?"

"For sure. We had a great night," Gazza stated enthusiastically.

Mitch laughed. "I'm pretty sure it was after class you enjoyed most," he said, causing both Brad and Gazza to chuckle sheepishly.

After waving off the guys, Mitch's eyes shifted

to the quiet Lore who seemed to have drifted off to sleep with his head resting against the jug in his lap.

Ten long minutes passed before the girls reappeared. Becca had her arm wrapped around a very pale looking Stacy, while Natasha followed along behind dancing to the Taylor Swift song that was playing.

Becca's eyes ran over the sedate-looking Lore before she focused on Mitch. "Are you going to be okay getting Lore in a taxi? I'm sure Brad and Gazza can help you." She spun on the spot as she obviously searched for them in the bar.

"They left already. Brad said he'd see you at work on Monday."

Becca flicked her eyes between Stacy and Lore, clearly torn about what to do.

Mitch offered Rebecca a sure smile. "I'll make sure Lore gets home safely. You look after Stacy."

Becca's shoulders sagged in relief. "Are you sure?"

"Yes. Go get her to bed before she starts throwing up again."

"Thank you," Rebecca said gratefully as she pressed a kiss to Mitch's cheek.

"No worries." He waved them off turning his attention back to Lore as he suddenly wondered how the hell he was going to follow through on his promise when he didn't even know where Lore lived. He swiftly regretted leaving Joey to input the students' forms tonight.

Mitch called a taxi before he hitched up his jeans and crouched beside Lore. "Lore? Are you ready to go home?"

Lore groaned and Mitch softly brushed his hair out of his eyes with the back of his hand to see him better. Lore leant into his touch. "Mmmm…"

Mitch cupped Lore's cheeks and gently lifted his head from its resting position on the jug. "Lore, do you think you can walk? There's a taxi on its way to take you home."

Lore's unfocused eyes locked onto Mitch's. "Home. Are you coming home with me?"

Mitch smirked. "Not tonight." Moving behind him, Mitch hooked his hands under Lore's arms and lifted him out of his seat. "Come on, let's go find that taxi."

Lore managed to move one foot in front of the other, with only a little support from Mitch, and by the time they made it outside there was a car waiting for them at the curb.

Mitch leant into the open passenger-side window to double check it was for them, but seeing no one else around he was pretty certain it was. "For Mitch?"

The driver nodded, which was good considering Lore was already attempting to slide into the back seat, only slightly hindered by the jug he had a death grip on.

"If he throws up, you'll have to pay for it to be cleaned."

Mitch gave the guy a confident smile as he slid into the backseat beside Lore. "He'll be fine. It's just a safety measure."

The driver narrowed his eyes but didn't argue anymore. "Where to?"

Mitch looked to Lore. "What's your address Lore?"

Lore gave Mitch a blank stare.

"Where do you live?" Mitch clarified.

Lore opened his mouth and closed it as a thoughtful look crossed his face. "Erm. Near the Uni."

Mitch shook his head. "That could be anywhere in the whole damn suburb," he muttered before rattling off his own address to the driver.

FOUR

LORE

As Lore snuggled into his bed he was accosted by an unfamiliar scent. A *delicious* unfamiliar scent. It was woodsy and sexy.

And all man.

His eyes popped open at the thought—he'd not had a man in his bed for a damn long time, sexy man scent did not belong on his sheets—and he regretted it the instant the bright sunlight hit his retinas.

He groaned and buried his head back into his pillow. After a few minutes he braved opening them again, only slower this time around.

Lore looked around a room he didn't recall ever seeing before and wondered how the hell he got there before panic flowed through him as he realised he must have gone home with someone. Lore wasn't one to have random hook ups. He was a dater; he always made sure to see a guy for a couple of weeks before he even thought about sleeping together.

The room didn't give much away about its owner. White walls and whitewashed pine furniture with blue checked bedding. There were a couple of beach-scene framed photos hanging on the walls, which Lore couldn't help but like. He recognised them as local, which had him wondering if he'd snagged himself a photographer.

Knowing he wasn't going to get any answers if he stayed hiding in the bedroom, he slipped out of the bed in just a pair of boxers and was relieved to see a pile of clothes folded on a white wicker chair by a chest of drawers, a note laid on top.

LORE,

I put your clothes in the wash. These should fit if you want to come out for food and painkillers.
M.

AS THE QUESTION of who M could be ran through his head he was suddenly plagued with a vision of him vomiting after getting out of a car, covering both himself and Mitch, his sexy self-defence teacher. His shoulders slumped as he was filled with shame. The one guy he was attracted to that seemed like him—may even actually be good for him—and he blew it by getting drunk and vomiting all over him.

Grabbing the clothes, Lore headed for what he could see was an en-suite, the door having been left wide open. After freshening up and getting dressed, he rubbed at his teeth with a finger of toothpaste to get rid of the stale taste he had in his mouth. It didn't do as good a job as a tooth-brush would have but it would do until he got home.

Lore cleared his throat as he stepped into the open plan kitchen-dining room and his eyes fell on Mitch who was standing over the stove wearing nothing but a pair of well worn ripped jeans.

Mitch gave him a wide smile and stepped away from the stove to push a glass of water and two pills across the island towards him. "Take those. I'm making pancakes." He glanced at Lore nervously. "I hope you like pancakes. If you don't, I can make something else." Mitch darted for the fridge.

Lore reached out to brush his arm, causing Mitch to freeze with his hand on the fridge door, his eyes dropping to Lore's hand. "I like pancakes, Mitch." Seeing this nervous, uncertain version of the put-together guy he'd met last night did a lot to settle Lore's nerves.

Mitch smiled and went back towards the stove. "Make sure you have those paracetamol."

Lore did exactly that, knowing the dull headache he had would only get worse if he didn't take the pills.

Mitch plated up the pancakes and carried the two dishes to the dining table. "What do you want to drink? Coffee? Tea? Juice?"

"Honestly, I'm easy." He caught sight of Mitch's smirk and realised what he'd said. "I mean…I'll have whatever you're having," he clarified, that nervous energy he'd managed to expel slowly creeping its way back in as he sat in front of one of the plates.

Lore observed as Mitch pulled a bottle of orange juice out of the fridge and placed it on the table along with two glasses.

Lore grimaced as thoughts of what his drunken self could have gotten up to last night flitted through his mind. "I didn't try anything inappropriate with you last night, did I?"

Mitch poured them both a glass then picked up his knife and fork. "You were the perfect gentleman. Well, if you don't count the part where you threw up on me, and then tried to undress me right there in the street."

Lore's eyes widened in surprise as his face heated. "Oh my god, kill me now."

"You weren't trying to get in my pants, just trying to get me out of my vomit-covered clothes. You meant well." Mitch let out a hearty laugh and Lore couldn't help but chuckle too.

A phone started ringing on the countertop and Lore belatedly recognised it as his own. "Shit, what time is it?" He darted out of his seat and picked up the phone not surprised in the least to see '*Mum*' flash across the screen. He was meant to be visiting her first thing this morning. The call went to voice-mail before he could slide to answer, so he waited for her to leave a message before trying to ring her back.

He gave Mitch an apologetic smile. "Sorry. It's my mum, if I don't call her back she'll send out a search party." It was true; she didn't need much of an excuse to send his brother out looking for him.

Mitch waved him off. "No worries. If you need some privacy you're more than welcome to use the bedroom."

Lore shook his head. "It's fine. I'll just tell her

I'll be a little late…well, later than I already am," he amended as he saw the time. *What was an hour more?*

The text came through telling him he had a new voicemail and he pressed his mum's name and held the phone up to his ear.

She answered almost immediately. "Lore?"

The worry in her voice instantly filled him with guilt.

"Are you okay? I was just about to send your brother to check on you."

"I'm fine, Mum." Lore rolled his eyes and turned away from the table. "Sorry I didn't come as planned but I was out late last night and crashed at a friend's. I forgot to set my alarm."

Lore's mum sighed. "Okay, you'll be here for lunch, won't you?"

"Yes. I'll be there for lunch. I promise."

"See you soon." Her voice was back to the cheery one Lore liked to hear from his mother and it did a good job of washing away the guilt over worrying her. She disconnected the call and he placed his phone on the table as he sat down to tuck back into his pancakes.

Mitch gave him a guilty look. "I think I may be to blame for you being late. I turned your alarm off. I'd dumped it beside the couch with mine when I went to sleep and just blindly turned it off thinking it was mine." He rubbed at the back of his neck.

Lore swallowed his mouthful of pancake and poured a little golden syrup on the next one. "Don't worry about it, I was out for the count and probably would have slept through it anyway." He filled up his fork and paused with it raised in front of his mouth. "By the way, these pancakes are so good," he stated before taking the bite off his fork.

Mitch's cheeks turned pink and he didn't make eye contact, leaving Lore to think he must have been embarrassed at the compliment. "Thanks. It's a secret family recipe."

"Wait. You slept on the couch?" Lore blurted out, belatedly registering what Mitch had said.

"Yeah. Did you think we'd...?" Mitch left the sentence hanging as he gave Lore a wide-eyed stare.

"No. I just... This place must have more bedrooms, I figured you'd be in one of those." Lore waved his arms gesturing towards the multitude of closed doors going off the open plan living area that he'd assumed a couple to be bedrooms.

Mitch nodded. "Ah, well, yeah it's a three-bedroom-house but the spare rooms don't actually have beds in them. It's not like I ever have guests so it's one of those things I've never gotten around to sorting out."

Lore felt awful. "You should have thrown me on the couch."

"Honestly, the couch is comfier than the bed anyway. I often sleep on it."

Lore knew he lied even though he hadn't even sat on the couch. The bed he'd woken up on was as soft as a cloud and covered in Mitch's scent.

"Well, thanks." Lore gave Mitch a grateful smile, hoping to convey how appreciative he was.

They ate the rest of their breakfast in a comfortable silence, neither of them feeling the need to fill it.

Lore gazed at Mitch as he crossed the room

with his empty plate and glass, placing them in the sink. His jeans were snug over his round arse, making Lore wish he wasn't there just because he'd gotten ridiculously drunk the night before. He let his eyes roam over Mitch's back, following the movement of his muscles as he made quick work of cleaning the dishes.

Lore grabbed his own dirty dishes and took them over to the sink. As he approached Mitch he had the sudden urge to place a kiss against the soft flesh on the curve of Mitch's shoulder.

Thankfully, Mitch chose that moment to turn and take Lore's plate and glass away before he could do something so foolish. Although, Lore couldn't stop his eyes eating up the smooth, hard chest he was now faced with.

"If you keep looking at me like that I won't be able to keep behaving."

Lore stared wide-eyed at Mitch's words as his heart beat in his chest erratically.

Mitch liked him.

This magnificent specimen of a man in front of Lore actually liked him…and wanted to do naughty things to him.

"Behaving is overrated."

Mitch's lips twitched at his statement.

Deciding he was never going to have this opportunity again Lore crushed his mouth against Mitch's as he closed the space between them.

There was a clatter of crockery and Mitch's hands were suddenly grabbing at Lore's hips, tugging him forward until their bodies were pressed together.

Seizing the moment, Lore ran his hands up the

delectable chest he'd been eyeing only minutes ago, feeling Mitch's nipples pebble beneath his fingertips as he brushed over them.

Mitch's tongue teased his lips and he was soon opening up to him, wanting to take whatever he was willing to give.

Someone moaned and Lore didn't know which of them it was. He didn't care either. He just wanted more.

His hands slid down to Mitch's jeans and he fumbled as he tried to blindly undo the button.

Avicii's *Hey Brother* started playing full blast, causing them to abruptly break apart.

Breathing heavily, Mitch glanced around the room, clearly looking for where the music was coming from.

Lore belatedly realised it was the ringtone he had set for his brother. The room suddenly fell into silence and all Lore could hear was their heavy breathing and the beating of his own heart.

"Fuck! I'm sorry." Mitch roughly ran a shaky hand through his hair as he stepped around Lore, his eyes darting everywhere and seemingly avoiding Lore's.

Lore knew what that meant. Whatever lusty haze had led to their moment of passion had certainly disappeared and if Mitch's actions were anything to go by, he was already regretting what they'd just done.

For the first time ever, Lore was actually grateful for his brother ringing during such a critical moment.

"No. Mitch, you've got nothing to apologise for.

I threw myself at you. I'm the one that should be sorry."

Mitch shrugged as he made his way towards his bedroom. "I'm gonna get changed and then I'll drop you off wherever you need to be. I'm guessing that was your mum again. We wouldn't want her worrying," he called as he disappeared out of sight, leaving Lore standing in the middle of the kitchen wishing he could start the day again.

Maybe even redo yesterday, too, while he was at it.

FIVE

MITCH

THE SILENCE in the car was deafening and Mitch couldn't stop thinking about the feel of Lore's mouth against his.

His hands fumbling with his jeans.

Fuck! He shouldn't be having these thoughts. He could never have someone like Lore.

He didn't deserve him.

Mitch pressed at a button on the radio, hoping the noise would distract him from his chaotic thoughts. An Ed Sheeran song came on and his traitorous mind immediately placed Mitch in Ed's shoes and had Lore as the love interest he was singing about. Feeling safer with his previous thoughts he plunged them back into silence, turning the radio off again.

"Do you have something against Ed Sheeran?"

He could see Lore watching him out the corner of his eye and it took all his willpower not to look. "Just that song," he lied.

Lore sighed and Mitch waited for him to say

something, perhaps defend the song, but he obviously decided to keep his opinion to himself.

Mitch turned onto the street Lore had given him and slowed his speed as he waited for the house to be pointed out since Lore hadn't bothered giving him the street number.

"It's that one with the red Colorado on the drive," Lore stated, nodding toward the Holden parked on the left about four houses from them.

The house was a nice sized two storey. There was a lake across the road surrounded by grass and trees. It was peaceful and Mitch wished he could go take a walk and enjoy it.

As they came to a stop Mitch couldn't help but wonder if this was the house Lore had grown up in. *Had he played near the lake with his mum telling him to not go too close to the water's edge?*

Lore cleared his throat, causing Mitch to turn his attention to him.

His gaze fell on Lore's lips and he instantly remembered how soft they were before he flicked them up to lock on Lore's eyes... Eyes that weren't hiding the sadness in them.

Sadness Mitch hadn't noticed before.

"Thanks for the lift."

"No worries. I was going to head out anyway." It was another lie, but once the words were out of his mouth he decided he'd head to the gym and do some of the paperwork that needed catching up on. Joey had been on at him saying they needed to take on a receptionist, but Mitch knew they were all things he could do and he had the time. The gym was his life now.

Lore opened the door but paused before

moving to get out, making Mitch's breath catch in his throat.

Was he going to make another move?

"Thanks for lending me the clothes, I'll bring them to self-defence next week," Lore announced.

Mitch was surprised to feel disappointed as Lore slipped out the car, even though he was the one that had freaked out when they'd gotten carried away back at his place. He wasn't interested in a relationship or even a fling, so why was there a knot in the pit of his stomach at the thought of Lore not attempting to make another move?

His body was a traitor.

"I'll be sure to take yours to the gym, too."

Lore gave him a last grateful smile before he pushed the car door shut and made his way up the drive without a backward glance.

Mitch felt like a sap watching him right up until he stepped into the house and closed the front door, but he couldn't help it. He was curious to find out if Lore would have a quick look back. They always did say curiosity killed the cat.

He sighed, suddenly feeling miserable as he flicked his indicator on before driving off from the curb.

THE HUMMING NOISE of the shredder seized and Mitch blindly reached for the next form on the desk only for his fingers to be met with the wooden desktop. He tore his eyes away from the floor where he'd been staring in a trance, thinking of nothing but that kiss he'd shared with Lore, and searched the desk for the papers he thought he still had left. The desk was empty.

The office door burst open and Joey stepped into the room. "Dammit, Mitch. Why can't you answer your damn phone?"

Mitch frowned and jumped up from his seat, immediately forgetting the task he'd been doing. "What's wrong? Is it your Mum?" Mitch asked, suddenly worried about her.

Joey stormed across the room and unplugged the shredder, tucking it back under the desk where it belonged. *"Is it Mum?"* He gave Mitch a look that didn't need words.

One that unmistakably said *'Are you stupid?'*

"Yes, it's Mum. She's done nothing but yell at me for the last hour for not looking after you properly since you obviously have something bothering you, so much that you didn't turn up for lunch like you were meant to."

Mitch slapped a hand against his forehead. "Shit. I completely forgot."

Joey rolled his eyes. "Clearly." He pulled a paper bag from behind his back and placed it on the desk. "Mum told me to give you this so you aren't drinking on an empty stomach."

Mitch frowned and Joey went on.

"She knows we keep that bottle of rum in the drawer for emergencies, and she knew you wouldn't miss lunch for anything less than an emergency."

Mitch ran a hand through his hair and—because he hadn't bothered putting any product on it that morning—it flopped right back against his forehead. "Has she got cameras in here or something?"

"Oh god, I hope not. I'm praying it's just mothers' intuition." He walked over to the drawer and pulled out the bottle of Captain Morgan's and two glasses they kept there. "But, we're here to discuss you and I have a feeling it's got something to do with that guy you couldn't seem to take your eyes off last night."

Mitch dropped his head into his hands with a groan. He still couldn't believe he'd been that obvious. He reached out for the glass Joey had just filled, but before he could get a solid grasp Joey snatched it away.

"Nah uh. Not until you've eaten that sandwich. I'll be in all kinds of trouble if I take you home smashed and having not talked through your problems."

Mitch made a show of opening the bag and having a large bite out of the egg salad sandwich. As he swallowed the first mouthful his stomach grumbled and he was desperate to have another bite, suddenly realising he was starving.

After watching Mitch devour one half of the sandwich his mum had made with only a few bites, Joey slid the glass across the desk to his friend. "You get one, then you need to talk."

Mitch took the glass with a nod and knocked it back. "I barely know him, but I like him." He took another bite.

"I don't see any problems there," Joey pointed out.

"Being in the same room as Lore… I forget."

Mitch whispered the last two words, unable to admit it any louder. "I shouldn't be able to forget."

Joey poured Mitch a second glass and downed his own. "You're allowed to forget, Mitch. You're allowed to have moments of happiness."

"I shouldn't ever forget. I fucking killed some-one!" Mitch raised his voice and, as much as he knew his friend didn't deserve his anger, he couldn't hold it back.

"Do you need me to dig out the coroner's report again?" Joey offered and Mitch shook his head. "Because I fucking will. Boone's death is not on you. He should never have been fighting that night. He knew that, that's why he kept his blackouts from everyone that could stop him fighting. The cerebral haemorrhage was avoidable if only he'd had some sense, but his need to win the belt was more important to him than his health was."

Mitch had read the report a number of times but no matter what words were on it, he still felt his fist connecting with Boone's head before he watched Boone drop to the floor and couldn't help but shoulder the blame.

"Over the last year I've watched my mate disap-pear into himself and it kills me. You need to find a way to live with this because wasting your life isn't good for anyone. Tell me something, does this guy like you as much as it looked like he did?"

Mitch's stomach flipped at the question because dammit...yes, he thought so. And he admitted as much with a nod. "I think so."

Joey topped up both their glasses, as Mitch scrunched up the paper bag on the desk and threw it in the bin in the corner of the room.

"Then promise me one thing." He offered out a glass to Mitch, who took it suddenly wary of what Joey might ask of him next. "You'll ignore that self-sacrificing voice in the back of your head and you'll give things a go with this guy… For me."

Mitch could have easily said 'yes' to that request and blown it off later, but with Joey adding that *'for me'* on the end… If he agreed he had to mean it. After taking a deep breath, and a moment to think, he realised Joey was right. He had to give this a go because otherwise he'd only come to have a lifetime of regrets when he looked back on this in ten years time.

With a quick sharp nod he clinked his glass with Joey's. "Promise."

SIX

LORE

LORE PULLED the phone away from his ear and glanced at the screen for confirmation that the number really was the number he'd called a few days before for the gym.

It was one and the same.

"Lore? Are you there?" Mitch's voice called faintly through the speaker.

He pressed the phone back to his ear. "Yes. Sorry. I was just…" He didn't know what to say. Mitch had just asked him out on a date. The same Mitch that had freaked out when they'd kissed several hours ago. "Are you sure?"

Mitch laughed, sounding nervous, which eased Lore's own jitters.

"I know, I didn't really give you the best impression earlier but I'd love it if you could forget about that and let us start fresh."

Lore took a moment to process Mitch's words, but he already knew there was only one answer. "Yes. I'd love to."

"Brilliant. Are you free tonight?"

It was Lore's turn to laugh. "You're eager." He glanced through his mum's kitchen window as he paced the back yard. It was the only place he could take a phone call without the whole family trying to eavesdrop. "Yeah, I was planning on leaving mum's soon."

"How about I pick you up from there at six-fifteen?" Mitch offered.

That was ten minutes away. "I'm still wearing your clothes and I don't have anything here to change into." Lore glanced down at the shirt and sweatpants in question and as much as he enjoyed wearing them he knew they hung off him since he didn't have the muscles Mitch had. His mum had been ecstatic that he'd come in wearing another guy's clothes. She'd almost run out to call Mitch in, but Lore had managed to block her way to the front door, and by the time she'd run around the back Mitch was already halfway down the street.

"I'm not really dressed to go out either..." Mitch paused and Lore guessed he must have been thinking. "What if we just grab a takeaway and head to one of our places to watch a movie on Netflix or something?"

Lore grinned to himself. "Netflix and chill sounds good to me," he admitted. He heard the distinct chuckle of his brother behind him and the words he'd just said registered in his mind. *Wasn't 'Netflix and chill' a euphemism for sexy times?*

Lore wanted the ground to swallow him. He'd only meant he'd much rather spend time with Mitch in private because he'd be able to relax and be himself more without the added worry of making a fool of himself in public. Not because he expected them to have sex.

"That's settled then," Mitch stated, obviously not catching on to Lore's error in choice of words, or perhaps he didn't mind the assumption. "See you soon," he added before disconnecting the call.

Lore stared at the home screen of his phone while he processed the fact that he had a date. Something he hadn't had in a while.

"So…Netflix and chill, hey?" Cormac questioned. Lore didn't even need to see his brother's face to know he was grinning ear to ear.

"Oh, don't, Mac," Lore groaned. "I feel like a big enough idiot as it is, I don't need you making it worse."

Mac laughed. "Fine, be a fun spoiler." Mac leant his backside against the picnic table on the deck as Lore slid onto one of the benches. "But seriously, you've got a date?"

"Yeah."

His brother cocked his head. "Is he gonna need hunting down in a few weeks time like the last pompous dick you dated?"

Lore rolled his eyes. "No. I'm pretty sure this one's a good guy. And if I'm wrong, you won't wanna hunt him down. He's a boxer."

Mac gave him a look of mock hurt, holding a hand over his heart. "You don't think your big brother can take him on?"

"Not a chance in hell."

Mac smirked. "Now I'm really intrigued to meet this guy."

The back door opened, catching their attention, as their mother's head appeared through the opening. "I wondered where you two were hiding. Our show's about to start, are you coming in?"

Lore grimaced. His mother loved their Saturday nights together and he was going to have to leave early. He'd not even thought about that when he'd told Mitch he'd about his plans. He was too excited at the prospect of Mitch liking him and actually wanting to date him to think about things like his mother's feelings.

"Mum, I'm sorry but I have to leave early."

"Yes. Our Lorcan has a hot date. He's a boxer, apparently. I was just getting all the details."

Lore glared at his brother as his mum's eyes filled with glee. Telling his mum the smallest piece of information like that meant she'd be digging for anything she could get, every single time Lore spoke to her. She'd never give up until Lore told her it was over.

"Oooh. Is he the boy who dropped you off earlier? It must be serious if you're wearing his clothes and you can only bear to be parted for a couple of hours before you have to catch up again."

Lore sighed. There she went, already running off with a fairy-tale ending. "Mum, it's not like that. I told you I was too drunk to get home last night, and he let me crash at his place. My clothes were in his washer this morning when I had to come here. That's all."

"But you're going on a date tonight," she stated, like that meant everything.

"Yes, but it might be awful and never happen again. So let's just drop it for now, okay?" Lore's mum sharply turned her head away, looking through the house as if she'd heard something.

"Oh, that must be him," she called out cheerfully as she headed into the house.

Lore's stomach did a somersault as he flew up from the bench and ran down the side of the house, heading for the gate which led to the front yard, knowing if he moved quickly enough he'd maybe just make it before his mother could answer the door and invite Mitch in.

Lore skidded to a halt on the stones behind Mitch, who spun at the noise just as the front door opened.

"Lore?" Mitch's eyes ran over Lore before drifting to the direction Lore had come from, obviously looking for a threat that Lore must be running from. His eyes narrowed and that was when Lore knew his brother had followed him.

Which was a no brainer really, of course he'd want a front row seat to his mother grilling Lore's date.

"Yep. Gee, look at the time. We best go or else we'll be late." Lore announced, hoping Mitch wouldn't call him out on his lie since Mitch was even earlier than he'd said he would be. Lore hooked an arm with Mitch's and tried to move him towards the car, only his date was too strong and he didn't seem to be going anywhere.

"Are you okay?" Mitch questioned.

"Hi, I'm Beth, Lorcan's mother. Would you like to come in…?" She pinned Mitch with a stare as she left the sentence hanging while waiting for an introduction.

Lore knew his chance to run was over but he could still save Mitch from the Spanish inquisition if he played his cards right. "Mum, this is Mitch.

We'd love to stay and chat but we really do have to be somewhere."

Mitch reached out his hand, and when Beth placed hers in his, he lifted it to his lips and placed a gentle kiss on it. "Pleased to meet you Mrs Col—"

"Beth. Please, call me Beth."

"Beth." Mitch gave her a smile that had not only her swooning but Lore, too.

Lore tightened his grip on Mitch's arm, to help keep himself grounded. He'd always heard of people talking about someone having a killer smile but he'd never exactly seen one himself. Now he could say he had.

Jesus, he was dating the hottest guy known to mankind.

SEVEN

MITCH

MITCH COULDN'T TAKE his eyes off Lore as he settled back into the corner of the sofa, his glass of
cider in hand. When they'd stopped off to pick up
their takeaway, they'd also slipped into the bottle
shop since Mitch knew he didn't have anything de-
cent to drink with dinner, and Lore had chosen a
fruity cider.

Mitch lifted his drink to his lips, taking a tenta-
tive sip. Having never tried the stuff before he was
wary of it not being to his taste, but he was pleas-
antly surprised as he took a larger mouthful. "This
stuff is pretty good."

Lore smiled. "I told you it was, but you didn't
trust me."

"In future I will take your word on everything,
okay?"

Lore chuckled at Mitch's words and he loved
the sound. It sent warmth shooting through him.
Lore narrowed his eyes. "So, tell me something.
Why don't you fight anymore?" I'd never followed

the sport but Mitch and his story had been all over the news after the fight, and as soon as he opened the gym and started advertising the self-defence lessons the media picked it all back up again. So I, and no doubt everyone else who'd joined up, knew exactly who our instructor was.

"Jesus. Jump straight in with the hard questions, hey?" Mitch sighed as he thought his answer through. It wasn't like Lore couldn't find out if he wanted. The Internet was full of theories, some spot on, others drastically far-fetched. Mitch wanted Lore to hear the truth and he wanted to be the one to tell him. So, despite his words, he was grateful for the hard question.

"The opponent in my last fight died in the ring and, as much as I was in no way at fault, I can't risk the chance of it happening again."

Lore nodded his acceptance and Mitch felt his shoulders sag as all the tension left his body. Anyone that had ever brought up the subject of him fighting always told him that he was too good to give it up. It was such a relief to have someone listen and just accept his decision. "Thank you."

Lore frowned. "For what?"

"Acceptance. You are the first person that hasn't tried to get me back in the ring when we've spoken about me no longer fighting."

Lore leant forward, placed his hand on Mitch's knee, and gave it a gentle squeeze. "Only you can decide what's right for you in regards to that, Mitch. Nobody else."

Mitch suddenly found himself tugging Lore into his lap, his mouth crushing against soft lips that had parted on a sigh of surprise.

Lore's hand slid around Mitch's neck and into the hair at the base of his skull, giving it a gentle tug and causing their mouths to part. "Are you sure you want it this time?" Lore's eyes bored into Mitch's searching for an answer. "Because if we do this there's no walking away. I can't have a repeat of this morning."

Mitch wanted it. He wanted it more than he'd ever imagined. His eyes dipped to Lore's lips for a split second before lifting back to his eyes. "I want this." He shook his head. "No running this time. I promise."

Lore took a moment to eye him before their lips were once again mashed together. This time Lore's tongue probed for entrance and, as soon as Mitch gave him access, he fought for dominance.

Lore's arse ground against Mitch's dick and Mitch didn't know if it was due to Lore, or the hands he was gripping Lore's hips with, but he didn't care one bit. It felt so fucking good and he needed more of it.

Mitch pulled his mouth away. "Fuck. We need to move this somewhere else. I need…"

"More," Lore finished as they both gasped for breath.

Slipping off Mitch's knees, Lore pulled him off the sofa by the T-shirt he had fisted in his hands. Once they were both stood to their full heights, Mitch drew Lore against his body, taking his lips once again in a passionate kiss. He couldn't get enough of them: their softness, their taste. They were all too perfect.

Mitch blindly walked Lore through the house

never breaking the kiss, not even when Lore grunted into his mouth as they backed into things.

Once they made it to the bedroom, Mitch shoved Lore onto the bed. "Strip," he ordered as he started ripping his own clothes off.

"If I wasn't so desperate to have you I'd have fun undressing you," Lore announced as he tugged at his own clothes, throwing them across the room once he freed himself from their confines.

Mitch paused at the end of the bed as he took in the sight before him. A very naked Lore spread out across the bed, his long hard cock leaking pre-cum as he oh-so-slowly ran his hand over it. Mitch fisted his own erection, giving it a gentle squeeze.

"As much as I love the sight of you with your cock in your hand, there'll be plenty of time for that later. Right now, I need you to get over here and fuck me."

Mitch's heart soared at Lore's admission. Although he wouldn't have minded bottoming if that was what Lore had wanted, he really needed to pin Lore to the bed and be inside him.

Climbing onto the mattress took him no time at all and he was soon leaning over Lore, his cock brushing against the flesh of Lore's stomach as he reached into the bedside table to pull out some lube and a condom.

Throwing the condom on the bed he squirted some lube on his fingers, being sure to slick them thoroughly, before kneeling back on his haunches and running a knuckle teasingly over Lore's hole. He felt it pulse under his fingers before he pressed a little harder, slipping one inside.

Lore groaned and it was the sexiest noise Mitch had ever heard.

He dipped his head and wrapped his mouth around Lore's cock, which he was still stroking leisurely.

"Oh fuck!" Lore cried out.

As much as Mitch had wanted to get to the fucking, the noises Lore was making had him taking his time. It was now suddenly his mission to draw as many of them out of Lore as he could.

Running his tongue up Lore's shaft he swirled it around the head and, at the same time, he pressed a second finger against Lore's hole. It slipped in without resistance and he made sure to take the time to stretch him as he sucked his cock deep into his throat.

"I'm gonna…" Lore shoved at Mitch's shoulder in an effort to lift him off his dick but, the second Mitch felt it pulse in his mouth, he doubled his efforts, swallowing around it. "*Mitch!*"

After swallowing down the last drops of cum, Mitch released Lore's cock as he pulled his fingers free. He smiled at the whimper that fell from Lore's mouth and crawled his way up Lore's body, pressing gentle kisses against his flesh as he went.

His hipbones. His bellybutton. A nipple.

He licked a line from one nipple to the other, before pressing a kiss there and lifting himself to be at eye level with Lore, making sure not to drop his whole weight on the satiated body beneath him.

"You gonna fuck me now?" Lore mumbled.

Mitch pressed a lazy kiss against Lore's jaw, and then his lips, before acknowledging his question. "That depends, do you think you can handle a good fucking?"

"There's only one way to find out," Lore stated and Mitch didn't need any more encouragement.

Tearing open the condom and suiting himself up in record time, he lined himself up and sunk into Lore, pressing him into the mattress having suddenly forgotten all about keeping his weight off the man.

Lore's hands snaked around Mitch's back, his short nails pressing into his shoulder blades as he pulled Mitch impossibly closer.

Surrounded by Lore, his arms, his flesh, and his scent, Mitch knew he'd found something that could truly make him happy.

Lorcan Cole.

EIGHT

LORE

THERE WAS a warmth against Lore's back that had him stretching and kicking the covers off in the same movement. He had no sooner separated from the furnace than he found himself encased in it once again.

As he came to he realised that the heat was Mitch and a grin spread across his face as he remembered the previous night's activities, giving him delicious aches in all the right places. They'd had the best sex of his life and he couldn't wait to have a repeat of it.

A loud noise came from Mitch's phone on the bedside table and Mitch groaned as he blindly reached for it. "Ugh. Is it that time already? It doesn't feel like I've had a full night's sleep."

Lore laughed as he turned in Mitch's arms to face him, pressing a kiss to a hard chest he'd become pretty well acquainted with. "That's because you *haven't* had a full night's sleep."

Mitch stroked up the length of Lore's back with his fingertips. "And whose fault might that be?"

Lore smirked. "I'm pretty sure you were the one who yanked me across the couch and into your lap."

"Oh, fine. It was my fault. Although…" Mitch ground his erection against Lore's between them. "If I call in sick, we could spend the day having a repeat of last night."

"Mmm…" Lore groaned, closing his eyes as he enjoyed the feel of his cock rubbing against Mitch's. Needing to be the adult he was he forced his eyes open and stilled Mitch's ministrations with a hand on his hip. "As much as I'd like to say yes, I've got a presentation at work today so I can't take the day off."

Mitch dropped his head and pressed a kiss to Lore's mouth before pulling back a fraction. "Okay. But how about we do something tonight? Dinner? A movie? Both?"

"I'll do anything as long as we can come back here again afterwards," Lore stated, nervousness showing in his voice despite the confidence of the words themselves. He was never forward but there was just something about Mitch that made him break out of his shell of safety.

Mitch grinned. "I'm more than happy with that answer," he stated before taking Lore's lips in a dominant kiss. Lore opened to him so glad he hadn't managed to turn this sex god off with his up-front answer.

Mitch pulled away far too soon for Lore's liking, but he knew it was necessary because if they kept on kissing Lore's restraint would have caved and they would have ended up staying in bed. And the meeting he had at work wasn't something he could miss. A huge contract relied on his presentation and, if he managed to snag it, Lore was in for a large commission. He could really do with the money too, since his roommate had moved out and he still hadn't found someone else suitable.

Lore sat up and perched on the edge of the bed as he looked for his clothes. He knew he had to go home before heading into work so the sooner he left the better. Glancing at his watch he mentally kicked himself for not setting his own alarm for half an hour earlier.

A deliciously naked Mitch appeared before him with Lore's clothes held out in his hand. "Are these what you're looking for?"

His eyes seemed to be locked on to Mitch's semi-hard, and very tempting, cock which happened to be just at his eye level. Feeling his own stir at the sight he tore his gaze away raising it to meet Mitch's amused brown orbs. "Thanks," he said, his face flushing at the thought of being caught ogling Mitch as he took the offered clothes.

A gentle knuckle brushed over his flaming cheek. "How about you jump in the shower first since you'll probably need to head home before work? I'd much rather shower together but I'm afraid we'd get carried away and you'd end up late for your meeting," Mitch admitted with a smirk.

Lore felt his lips turn up into a grin of their own as he slipped his feet into his boxers and jeans before standing and tugging them up. "Thanks, but I think I'll grab a shower at home."

Mitch nodded before striding over to his chest

of drawers. "Give me five and I'll drive you home." Mitch marched into the bathroom without waiting for Lore's reply, closing the door behind him.

The sound of running water hit Lore's ears and he had to distract himself with fastening his jeans, pulling on his shirt, and hunting for his phone because all his mind wanted to do was picture a naked Mitch all wet and soapy; and that would not get him to work anytime soon.

AFTER MITCH HAD DROPPED him at home, Lore had the quickest shower of his life before driving to work faster than legally allowed. He spent the rest of the day in a bit of haze, thoughts of Mitch not far away. Lore left his meeting wondering how the hell they'd managed to pull off the contract, because he blundered through his jingle and presentation. He must have done something right though because the guy had signed the contract before he even left the room, which was usually unheard of—the client nearly always took the contract home to read over it before signing. There was still a fourteen-day grace period, but he seemed so set on signing immediately that Lore couldn't see the client pulling out.

As soon as Lore walked through the door of the gym he found himself under interrogation.

"What exactly are your intentions towards Mitch?"

Lore stared wide-eyed at the blond guy behind the counter unsure on what to say. The only answer flowing through his mind in that moment was 'to *fuck him a number of times'* and somehow Lore knew that wasn't the answer Joey was looking for.

"Jesus, Joey. Are you trying to scare him off?" Mitch's voice had Lore relaxing instantly, knowing there was no chance he'd be expected to answer Joey's question with Mitch present.

Joey laughed. "If a question like that is enough to scare him away then I don't know if he's worth keeping."

"*Joey!*" Mitch admonished before giving Lore an apologetic look. "He's not usually this much of a dick, I swear. Let's get out of here before he says something worse."

Lore gave Mitch a dumbfounded look. "You think he could come up with something worse?"

Mitch laughed. "It's Joey." He slipped his arm over Lore's shoulder and Lore settled into his side happily. "Stick around long enough and you'll realise he can manage much worse."

Leaving both their cars in the car park Mitch led them down the street in silence. It wasn't awkward so Lore soaked up the feel of Mitch's muscles flexing around his neck and against his side. He'd never been so hyperaware of someone else body before and that thought made him giddy.

"Do you like pizza?" Mitch asked, breaking the silence. "There's a new pizzeria that opened last week that brought some freebies into the gym on opening day, and they make *the* best pizza."

"I love pizza." After a second's hesitation Lore decided to break the ice. "Since we are talking pizza, I have a question for you. Pineapple. Does it belong on pizza or not?"

"Oh good god. I've known that question to destroy the best of marriages." Mitch's voice was filled with mock terror. "Are you sure you want to ask that so early in our relationship?"

The way Mitch labelled what was happening between the two of them with so much ease had Lore's heart beating in a manic rhythm. *Relationship.*
We're in a relationship.

All Lore could do in reply was nod, his mind happily stuck on that one magical word. He'd only known Mitch few days but for some reason Lore knew he wanted so much more from this guy than a casual hook up, and to hear the word 'relationship' come out of his mouth—that was like music to his ears.

"Okay. Well…" Mitch started, and Lore waited on tenterhooks, eager to hear the reply. Not that he would've been upset with one answer over the other because at the end of the day, everyone had different tastes. "I'm not fussed either way. If I'm given pizza with it on, I'll eat it. If it doesn't have it on, I wouldn't complain either."

Lore sighed, feeling a little disappointed with Mitch's non-answer. "Well that was very diplomatic of you. I'm not gonna lie. I'm a little underwhelmed with that."

Mitch chuckled. "Tell you what. Ask me again when I've had a drink or two and I might not be so diplomatic."

Lore grinned. "As long as I don't forget what I was meant to ask once I've had a couple of drinks. My memory isn't up to much on the best of days."

They were both laughing hard when they stepped into the pizzeria and Mitch led them straight to a booth. Once Lore was seated Mitch slid in the seat opposite.

Lore immediately missed the heat of Mitch's body warming his side and hoped they wouldn't be in here too long because he wanted to walk back to their cars, once again wrapped up in Mitch's body heat.

Lore didn't need to look at the menu. He knew what he wanted. It was the pizza he always got no matter where he ordered. Hawaiian. Also known as ham and pineapple. After Mitch's diplomatic response Lore was eager to see his reaction to the order. For now, he enjoyed the time he had taking in Mitch's defined jaw and the concentration lines between his brows as he read the menu.

Mitch lifted his eyes from the selection, immediately locking onto Lore's, having no doubt felt his stare trained on him. "Are you going to look at the menu?"

Lore shrugged. "I don't need to. I already know what I want."

Mitch frowned but soon gave Lore a suspicious look. "Hawaiian?" Lore nodded with a laugh and Mitch shook his head. "Why am I not surprised?"

Lore could tell by the sparkle in his eyes and the quirk to his lips that Mitch was only feigning disappointment.

The two of them talked all through dinner, barely noticing anyone else in the pizzeria. The conversation was easy and Lore was more than happy that they seemed to have some similar interests. He was yet to be convinced that Star Wars was better than Star Trek but they'd already agreed on a couple of marathon sessions to decide that one.

Mitch finished his pizza and Lore glanced down to look at his last two slices. Knowing there was no way he'd be able to eat them both he offered one to Mitch.

Mitch reached for it before pulling his hand back and eyeing the slice warily. "No thanks. I'm good."

Lore smirked as he gave Mitch a raised brow. "Be honest—how do you really feel about pineapple on pizza?"

Mitch's shoulders dropped in defeat. "Fine. Pineapple is a fruit, and fruit doesn't belong any-where near pizza." He rushed the words out in a hurry.

"Wow…Mitch, don't hold back." Lore held a fist to his chest faking heartbreak and they both burst out into laughter, drawing attention from other customers. Spotting the wandering eyes, Lore placed his napkin on the plate and gave Mitch a pointed look. "I guess we should make a move."

Mitch grimaced as he glanced around the room, obviously only just noticing the disruption they were causing. "That's probably best, the pizza is too good to risk getting banned." They both stood and headed for the door.

"Have a good night guys," Marvin, the man-ager, shouted as Mitch opened the door.

"Thanks," they both called out at the same time.

Lore's heartbeat kicked up a notch as Mitch threw his arm over Lore's shoulder once again. "Where to now?" Lore's voice wavered with nerves, as he gave Mitch a side-glance. He knew where he wanted to go but he didn't have the guts to be as forward as he had earlier in the day by saying 'let's get down to the good stuff'. Inhaling Mitch's cologne all the way through dinner meant he was now extremely desperate to get Mitch out of his clothes and into bed.

"Honestly?" Mitch asked as his long fingers stroked along Lore's collarbone. Lore nodded and Mitch carried on, "I can't stop thinking about getting you naked again."

Lore wanted to jump up and down with glee knowing Mitch was having the same struggles as he was. "Your place or mine?" he asked in a hurry.

"Which is closer?"

Lore laughed at Mitch's reply, loving how at ease he felt with this man. He'd never really had that before, and it was such a welcomed change.

MITCH

MITCH SHOOK thoughts of Lore naked beneath him out of his head. It was not something he should have been thinking about when he was at work, especially when he knew he had a spin class in five minutes. That wasn't something one wanted to do with a hard on. But his memories from the previous night were running on a loop and not helping him focus on work.

Hearing the bell above the door jingle, he shut down the accounts program on the computer and stood, knowing that although the trainer of the last spin class would have left the place ready to go he still felt he needed to be there before the customers settled in.

"Mitch doesn't do that anymore. I'd be happy to take you on."

Hearing his name through the open door, he picked up his pace as he crossed the small office. Curious to find out who was asking about him, Mitch's eyes fell on the ghost that had been haunting him day and night. His heart jumped into his throat at the sight.

Boone Carter.

Boone Carter was standing at the counter. *How was that even possible?* Boone had died in the ring over a year earlier and Mitch knew this for certain —he'd been his opponent after all.

He stumbled in the doorway and gripped the frame to keep upright as the world seemed to tilt on its axis.

"Fuck!" Joey called out leaping towards Mitch.

Mitch's vision started to blur as he felt solid hands grab on to his biceps and all sound seemed to melt away to nothing but a loud whooshing filling his head.

Boone. His stomach churned, as all he could focus on was that Boone was before him. Not just in his nightmares but right there in the flesh.

His arse hit a chair hard and a set of green eyes that were becoming all too familiar came into his line of sight, blocking the view of the man from his past. "Breathe." Lore's calming order had him instantly following the instruction and, with the hit of oxygen, he was assaulted with sounds that all seemed to come back at once.

"That's it, and again," Lore praised.

"B…Boone."

Lore flexed his fingers as they gripped his shoulders tightly. "Forget that for now. Just breathe."

Mitch did as he was told. Lore's warm, encouraging eyes were grounding him with every breath he took. Once he no longer felt like he was going to pass the fuck out he made to stand, only Lore, who still had a solid grip on his shoulders, wouldn't let him.

"Just sit for a bit longer. Please." The concern in Lore's eyes and the depth of his voice had Mitch complying. He'd clearly worried the guy and that was the last thing he wanted to do.

Mitch stretched to look around Lore. Something that looked like understanding crossed Lore's face and he took a step to the side. Mitch's eyes immediately landed once again on the man who started all this.

"How?"

The man shook his head. "I'm sorry, I didn't think. I'm not Boone. We are…" He frowned, "*were* identical twins."

Mitch's heart sunk and he didn't know how to process what he was hearing. His eyes flicked around the room landing on first Joey and then Lore, who both gave him a reassuring, if cautious, smile.

He suddenly felt like an idiot. He'd known Boone had a twin. Hell, he'd been in Boone's fucking corner in the ring. He shook his head. "I'm sorry. I feel like a dick."

"No. It's understandable. I forget we looked so alike to others. We never saw it. Neither did our family, mainly Mum. Dad was always getting us mixed up." The smile on the guy's face was hard not to return and Mitch felt himself smiling, even though his heart was hurting over the thought of what this man had lost. "Anyway." He shook his head dismissively. "Listen to me rambling on. I'm Wyatt." He offered his hand to Mitch.

After taking a deep breath he stood and strode

towards Wyatt, taking his hand in his own trembling one. "Mitch. Again, I'm sorry about…" He hooked a thumb over his shoulder and hoped that was enough because he really didn't want to go over what had happened back there.

Wyatt dropped his hand and waved him off. "Eh, forget it. And I know who you are. I actually came to see you."

Mitch's mind suddenly went back to what he'd heard as he was leaving the room. His eyes darted to the clock, belatedly remembering that he was on his way to run the spin class. "Shit. Spin class was meant to start fifteen minutes ago." He took a step forward, but a hand locked around his wrist. His eyes fell on Lore who was holding him back.

"Bev's taken the class," Joey stated. Mitch frowned, wondering what else he'd missed in those fuzzy moments. "Wyatt wants to fight and he wants you to train him."

Mitch felt the colour drain from his face this time; the warmth of Lore's hand was the only thing keeping him in the here and now.

"It's okay. I told him you don't train anyone. You don't even fight."

Mitch nodded, feeling numb. He couldn't understand why the thought of training someone would cause him such fear. It wasn't like he'd been training Boone. Wyatt gave him a reassuring smile at Joey's words but all he could see was Boone unconscious on the floor of the ring.

Lore's fingers slid down his wrist and interlaced with his own, grounding him once again. Fuck, he didn't deserve this guy. Mitch had no idea how someone he'd known for such a short time could affect him like that, but he couldn't dwell on that thought or his heart would be running double time for a whole other reason.

"Why don't you call it a day? There aren't anymore classes today and I can handle what little paperwork's left." The sympathy in Joey's eyes had Mitch nodding instantly.

He needed to get out of there. Out of that small space with a man who resembled his nightmares far too closely. Away from Joey and his pity filled eyes.

Lore tugged him towards the door without hesitation and Mitch was grateful he hadn't had to explain himself. The further away he got from the gym — and Wyatt — the clearer his mind became and, with that clarity, the guilt of what he'd done to Boone and his family pressed down harder than ever. Family who would only see their son or brother in the reflection of a mirror, the similarities in each other, and the photos they had hanging on the walls.

Mitch slipped into Lore's car without question; after all, he knew he was in no state to drive. His mind was far too distracted.

As Lore drove them down into the underground parking of an apartment block Mitch swung his attention to the man beside him. "Where are we?"

"My place." Lore shrugged. "You need to get out of your head and you probably won't be able to do that in your own space."

Mitch's heart sang. The fact that Lore knew what he needed, when Mitch hadn't even thought of it himself, spoke volumes. *How could one person understand another so well in such a short time?*

Mitch wondered if he'd have known what Lore needed if the situation had been flipped. He had a feeling he wouldn't, which only made his stomach churn and the thoughts about not deserving Lore come back double fold.

"Welcome to my humble abode."

While he'd been stuck in his head this time, Mitch had exited the car and walked up a flight or two of stairs on autopilot. He hadn't even noticed Lore had stopped to unlock a door.

Lore looked nervous when Mitch's eyes landed on him and he belatedly realised Lore was waiting for a reaction. Mitch focused his attention on the room before him, his gaze immediately falling upon a spectacular view of the Glass House Mountains in the distance.

"That's some view," Mitch stated, his voice full of awe.

"Stick around until sunset. It's magical." Lore's smile was warm and welcoming. It would be a lie if Mitch didn't admit he was tempted to stick around, but he also knew he'd be awful company and didn't want to make Lore deal with him any longer than necessary.

<h1 style="text-align:center">TEN</h1>

LORE

"CAN I?" Mitch nodded towards the sliding door leading to the balcony, a conflicted look on his face.

Lore nodded. "Go ahead. I'm gonna grab a cider. Do you want one?" Lore wasn't one to normally drink during the day unless it was with lunch but he felt like it was what Mitch needed to calm his nerves and he was certain Mitch wouldn't have one if he didn't.

"Sure. Thanks." Mitch shrugged, nonplussed. "I'm not planning on going back to work today and I didn't drive here," he explained.

Lore grabbed a six-pack out the fridge and took his time heading to the balcony, giving Mitch a moment to settle in. He'd let Mitch lead tonight; if he needed to talk, Lore would listen, but if he didn't he wasn't going to push.

Lore stepped out to find Mitch on the cane two-seater sofa. He placed the six-pack on the glass coffee table and after only a moment of hesitation, he settled into the plush cushions beside Mitch. If

Mitch had wanted to sit alone he would have sat in the single chair. Well, at least that was what Lore hoped anyway.

Taking two bottles out he offered one to Mitch and they both twisted the tops off, the hiss of air filling the quiet. After a minute or two Mitch broke the easy silence between them.

"I really thought it was him."

Lore glanced at the man beside him, taking in his profile — the long nose with a slight bump in it, and the strong jawline. Lore's hand itched to reach out and stroke along that jaw, making him wonder when he started to have thing for them. It wasn't something he had ever really noticed on a lover before.

Mitch's eyes were trained on the mountains in the distance but it was clear his mind was elsewhere. "It's stupid. I know he's dead but when I saw him…" He shook his head.

Lore reached out, placing his hand on Mitch's forearm. "It's understandable, Mitch. It really is."

Mitch placed his hand on top of Lore's and glanced across giving him a small smile that didn't quite reach his eyes. "Thanks. I don't know how, but you seem to know just what I need today when I don't even know myself."

Lore shrugged. "I'm talented like that."

Mitch chuckled which is exactly what Lore was aiming for and Lore took a sip of his cider.

He absentmindedly hummed a tune to a jingle he'd been working on that had been playing on his mind for days, the tune was so clear, but the words just weren't coming to him.

"What was that?" Mitch asked, curiosity obvious in his voice.

Lore gave Mitch a shy smile as he felt his face heat. "It's a jingle for an ad I've been working on. The tune seems to be haunting me but the words are nowhere to be found." He shook his head. "Actually that's a lie. I know they are there, I can all but feel them, but they seem to be just out of reach. You know like when you have something on the tip of your tongue but you just can't get it out."

Mitch nodded.

"It's like that."

Mitch placed his empty bottle on the table and turned in the chair to look at Lore in what must have been a more comfortable position. "Does that happen often?"

"All the time. It's just part of the process." Lore took a swig of his drink before swapping it for a fresh bottle and offering Mitch another.

"Thanks." Mitch said as he twisted off the top.

"It'll all fall into place eventually," Lore stated with an air of confidence. He was good at his job and he'd been doing it long enough to know what he said was the truth.

THE SUN HAD SET and there was a chill in the air, making Lore wish he'd purchased the outdoor heater he'd been eyeing up in the local hardware store last week. He and Mitch had been chatting easily for the last few hours and he hated to disturb the easy peace they had between them on the balcony, but he was cold and, if he was honest, he was hungry too.

"Is there anything you don't eat?" Lore asked as he tried to remember what he had in his fridge that he'd be able to make a quick meal out of. His apartment had started to feel like a little sanctuary and he didn't want to change that by going out for food.

Mitch frowned as he shook his head. "No, I'll eat pretty much anything, why?"

"Well, I don't know about you, but I missed lunch and I've had…" He took a moment to count the empty bottles on the table, "five bottles of cider. If I don't have something to eat soon I'll probably be falling over the balcony when I grab the next six pack."

"I'm tempted to say I wouldn't let you fall…" Mitch rubbed at the back of his neck with a palm, "but I'm feeling a little tipsy myself and couldn't guarantee my reflexes would be up to a promise like that," he stated with an accompanying nervous chuckle.

Lore stood. "That settles it. We need to eat," he said as he grabbed one of the now empty six packs off the table and stepped towards the sliding door, staying as far from the balcony edge as possible. He wasn't joking about feeling a little wobbly on his feet.

Bottles clanged together and he felt Mitch's body heat behind him, making it clear he'd picked up the remaining empties and was following Lore inside.

Whilst sitting outside chatting about shit, Lore had wanted nothing more than to touch Mitch, maybe even kiss him. And normally he probably would have at least attempted to make a move even if he still felt Mitch was way out of his league, but knowing the vulnerable state Mitch had been in earlier that day he hadn't wanted it turn things in that direction. He wanted Mitch to want him, but not just as a distraction and that was all it would be tonight.

It didn't take the two of them long to throw together a quick stir fry and thankfully they managed to keep all their fingers intact, even in their slightly inebriated states.

Lore filled two large glasses with cold water and placed them on the dining table where Mitch had set their places before turning to fetch the plates only to find Mitch behind him, said plates in hand.

Mitch grinned. "Figured I'd save you the trip."

"Thanks." The worry in Lore's chest eased as he weighed up Mitch and saw how much lighter the guy looked. The alcohol might have helped but Lore liked to think that the easy conversation and his company went a long way to helping too.

It only took a few bites of food and a good half glass of water before Lore started to feel himself sobering up. It was somewhat of a relief if he was being honest with himself because he didn't want to wake up with a hangover tomorrow, not when he'd booked in for an early self-defense class. It suddenly occurred to him that Mitch might not feel up to teaching that class. Not after everything that happened today.

"Will you be up for classes tomorrow?" Lore found himself asking before he could really think better of it, worriedly biting at his lip hoping he hadn't send Mitch back into his head again.

Mitch laughed. "Yes. I'd never live it down if I let a hangover get in the way of a class. Joey can be a dick like that."

"No, I was thinking about…" Lore left the sentence hanging, wishing he'd just gone along with Mitch's line of thinking.

"Ah. Today!" Mitch said, his face dropping as he caught on.

The atmosphere in the room changed and Lore wanted to kick himself for even speaking in the first place. Placing his knife and fork on the empty plate before him he downed the last mouthful of water in his glass, giving Mitch time he probably needed to think.

Mitch sighed. "I'll be fine. Joey and I have worked hard to get the gym to where it is. I can't let Wyatt's appearance ruin all that. Even if I feel like *I* don't deserve the success, I know for a fact that *Joey* does."

Knowing there wasn't anything he could say in reply that wouldn't cause Mitch to dwell on things more, Lore cleared away the plates and put them in the dishwasher so it would be ready to switch on when he went to bed. It was a little routine he'd gotten into the habit of thanks to his ex—he'd insisted on using it and now Lore couldn't seem to break himself of the habit, even when he barely managed to get it half full. Thankfully, with Mitch's company it was a little fuller.

"Do you want a coffee?" Lore shouted over his shoulder as he grabbed himself a cup from the cupboard, his hands paused over a second one. "Or tea," he added, suddenly realising Mitch might prefer that at night. Not everyone could drink caffeine so late.

"I'll take a coffee." Mitch's voice was so close Lore jumped and managed to knock a mug right off the shelf. He juggled but managed to catch it as Mitch chuckled. "Sorry, I didn't mean to scare you."

Lore clutched at his chest, feeling his heart racing under his palm while he gave Mitch an accusatory glare. "You're a freaking ninja."

"Hmm… I know you aren't exactly into sport but there is a huge difference between boxers and ninjas."

The playful glint Lore could see in Mitch's eyes had him stepping in close. "Huge, you say?"

Mitch grinned and, as much as Lore had worried about doing anything today, he knew whatever was going to happen wouldn't be because of the wrong reasons. "Oh yeah…" Mitch bit at his lip as though he was contemplating his next words. "I could show you how huge, if you want?"

Knowing he needed to keep this light and playful before he got hot, heavy and needy—because damn he'd wanted Mitch to jump his bones already but had a feeling if he showed Mitch how much, it'd only scare the guy away—he shrugged nonchalantly as he made a show of glancing at the clock on the wall. "I don't know…The Bachelorette starts in five minutes. Will it be worth it?"

Lore jumped as Mitch pinched his arse, the movement bringing them closer together; chest to chest.

Mitch brushed his lips against Lore's ear as he spoke. "You're a cheeky shit. Do you know that?"

Lore slid his hand between them, rubbing it over Mitch's crotch in the process. His own dick hardened at the feel of what was lying beneath the denim, ready for action. "I've been told it a time or two."

Mitch groaned. "I bet you have."

Their lips mashed together and Lore wasn't sure who had moved first. He didn't care either, as all thoughts that didn't involve getting naked as soon as possible fell from his mind.

Hands tugged at clothes and their tongues tangled, fighting for control of the kiss. Lore broke the kiss so he could pull Mitch's shirt over his head.

"Bedroom." Mitch stated before taking Lore's mouth in a bruising kiss once again.

Lore ran his hands over Mitch's chest, tweaking his pebbled nipples. Mitch groaned into Lore's mouth and Lore shoved his shoulders gently causing him to stumble back and effectively break them apart.

Mitch gave Lore a wounded look, obviously thinking Lore was having second thoughts.

"This isn't getting us any closer to the bedroom," he explained as he grabbed Mitch's hand and dragged him through the apartment, wanting nothing more than to spend the rest of the night exploring Mitch's muscular body.

ELEVEN

MITCH

TWO WEEKS HAD PASSED since the day Wyatt had walked into the gym, bringing back ghosts Mitch had thought he'd finally put to rest. Joey had taken him on, training him for some upcoming fight and he was in the gym more often than not. It would have been fine if only Mitch's heart would stop stuttering in his chest every time he laid eyes on the guy.

Mitch didn't freak out or think for even a second that it could be Boone, he wasn't that crazy. It was just his heart that didn't seem to be completely off the crazy train.

The smell of Lore's cologne had Mitch's head snapping up to the sight of him standing in the office doorway, his wet hair sticking out in all directions making him look freshly shower fucked.

"Hey…" was all Mitch could manage before he had to swallow. Lore took his breath away and he never seemed to see it himself which made him even more endearing to Mitch.

"Hi. I figured if I showered here before heading to Mum's I'd be able to meet you back here before you lock up. That is if you want to… I never thought, you might be sick of the sight of me and—"

Mitch strode across the room and cut Lore's rambling off with a kiss he'd meant to be demanding but, as their lips touched, it was like his mouth had a mind of its own, moving slow and sensually, stirring feelings he wasn't ready to analyse just yet.

After enjoying the kiss for far too long he pulled back. "I'd never get sick of you. Don't ever doubt that, okay?"

"I guess." Lore smiled shyly. "Okay," he added with a shrug.

Mitch cradled Lore's face with his palms. "I mean it, Lore. You brighten my life and I'd hate not seeing you as often as I do." Mitch pressed a hard kiss to Lore's lips but didn't linger. He had back-to-back spin classes in two minutes and knew Joey would be chasing him up any second if he didn't get his arse into the spin room.

Lore's phone rang and he jumped back. "That'll be Mac, he's picking me up and I'm not outside. I'll be back later then."

"I'll be looking forward to it all night. Enjoy dinner with your family."

Lore waved as he ran out the door, his phone ringing once again causing Mitch to laugh. Mac obviously didn't have patience like his brother did. He'd met the guy once or twice in passing but never actually had a conversation with him. Mitch was looking forward to getting to know Lore's family and Lore his. It wasn't something they'd discussed yet but Mitch was more than ready for it, things between them were getting serious—they spent more nights together than apart—and *meeting the parents* was the logical next step.

MITCH WIPED the sweat off his face and neck with a gym towel. The two back-to-back classes had taken it out of him more than he'd expected, making him realise that he needed to do some extra cardio. He'd been slacking off since meeting Lore, choosing to spend his early mornings cuddled into his warm body rather than sticking to his routine of running around the neighbourhood.

Knowing Lore would be arriving any minute he headed straight for reception, deciding on grabbing a shower when he got home—the added bonus to that would be Lore could join him. As he got closer the sound of voices reached his ears, voices he recognised as Joey and Wyatt.

"No, he's still pretty reserved with me to be honest. Freezes up for that split second when he sees me too. He probably doesn't even realise he's doing it," Wyatt stated.

Mitch hung back just outside the doorway. It wasn't right to listen but the fact that they were talking about him made him feel a little bit better about it.

Joey sighed. "He's still wracked with guilt. I wish I could just shake it out of him but he's not letting it go."

"I think...I think he needs to get back in the

ring." Wyatt's words grew in confidence as he finished the sentence clearly certain he knew what Mitch needed.

"Good luck with that. He hasn't even thrown a punch since…" Joey had left the sentence hanging but they all knew what he was talking about.

Since the day of the fight.

The day Boone died.

Anger pooled in Mitch's gut. He didn't need to get back in the ring. He didn't need to risk something like that happening again. And they had no right to discuss him like they were. Mitch felt like he needed to hold onto that guilt. If he didn't, wouldn't he forget what happened? Forget Boone even existed. Boone deserved to be remembered by Mitch, even if it was only through guilt.

Mitch stormed into the office as his anger bordered on rage. "I'd expect you of all people to want the person who caused Boone's death to feel something," he snapped, waving his finger at Wyatt.

"*Boone* caused his own death and that means the culprit can't feel anything. It certainly doesn't mean you—"

The bell above the door jingled, causing Wyatt to pause mid-sentence. Mitch was glad of it because he couldn't stand Wyatt's pitying tone. Lore glanced between the three guys and grimaced. "I don't know what I just disturbed but I can go back out if you want?" He hooked a thumb over his shoulder.

Mitch shook his head. "You're not disturbing anything. But I'm more than ready to go if you are?"

Lore frowned as he weighed Mitch up, but

agreed with a nod, not bothering to argue about whatever had concerned him.

Once outside Mitch took a deep calming breath and slipped his hand into Lore's, which had been hanging freely at his side. "What's the plan for tonight? Your place or mine?" Mitch asked as the strolled down the street.

"I don't care as long as you shower the minute we step in the door."

"I don't smell that bad." Dropping his head Mitch sniffed himself and quickly screwed up his face. "Ugh, maybe I do."

Lore laughed before nudging Mitch with his shoulder. "I kinda like you all sweaty anyway."

Mitch knew exactly what Lore was hinting at. They'd gotten plenty sweaty more than once or twice and not from being in the gym. Just the thought of rolling around between the sheets with Lore had him walking faster. "My place is closer," he said as he pulled a chuckling Lore along.

"Anyone would think you have some wicked plans you want to get to."

Mitch threw Lore a smirk over his shoulder, not slowing his pace in the slightest. "They may be wicked, but you're gonna love them."

TWELVE

LORE

MITCH'S MOUTH was on Lore's the second he'd turned from closing the door behind him. He was momentarily surprised but immediately opened up to Mitch at the brush of tongue across the seam of his lips. Lore loved Mitch's kisses. They were passionate and needy, and *always* a turn on.

Lore ran his hands up Mitch's arms, gripping at his shoulders as he broke the kiss. "You need a shower and food before we can take this any further."

"How about we take this into the shower? That way we kill two birds with one stone," Mitch offered as he leant in to carry on where they'd left off.

Lore looked at him with a raised brow. "And food?"

Mitch waved him off. "I can survive a little longer without food, but I won't survive waiting for you."

Lore couldn't believe it, but Mitch had said the only thing that could have won him over. After hearing that there was no way Lore was going to let Mitch shower alone. He grabbed Mitch's hand and pulled him towards the bathroom, unable to get there quick enough. "What are we waiting for?"

Mitch's laughter followed behind and Lore grinned from ear to ear all the way.

Lore spun around and crushed his mouth against Mitch's the second they'd made it into the bathroom. Mitch backed him towards the shower until Lore's back was pressed against the glass. He shifted without breaking the kiss and Lore heard the water start to spray. It was only then that Lore pulled back long enough to tug at Mitch's shirt and tear it over his head.

Mitch lifted the hem of Lore's shirt—saving him the trouble of reaching for it himself—and he raised his arms to comply. Once the shirt was out of the way Lore's fingers slipped into the waistband of Mitch's shorts.

"Someone's eag—"

Lore cut off Mitch's words with another kiss. Taking advantage of Mitch's surprised gasp by slipping in his tongue, Lore pushed Mitch's shorts over his hips and grasped his cock.

Mitch moaned into Lore's mouth before pulling back and taking a breath. "Fuck. I love your hands."

Lore worked Mitch's cock at the speed he'd quickly learned his lover enjoyed most. "Just my hands?"

"I might…need reminding about…the rest. *Oh god, Lore,*" Mitch said, his voice breathy.

Knowing Mitch was on the edge he released his cock. Mitch opened his mouth, to complain no doubt, but before he could say a word Lore gave him a pointed look.

"I want my cock inside you before you come and that can't happen until we get in there." He hooked a thumb over his shoulder indicating the shower.

Mitch moved quicker than Lore had ever seen him move. "What are you waiting for?"

Lore chuckled as he slid his own shorts and boxers down his legs and stepped out of them.

Mitch pulled him in for a quick wet kiss under the spray. He reached around Lore for something Lore couldn't see and pushed a bottle of lube into Lore's hands as he broke the kiss and turned his back on him. "I need you right now. And I won't last long."

Lore loved Mitch when he was needy. Hell, Lore loved all of Mitch's sides but *needy Mitch* was someone Lore was certain not many people got to meet, and fuck if that thought didn't make Lore feel like a king…

Lore slicked up his dick with plenty of lube, not wanting to hurt Mitch and knowing they wouldn't be spending time on prep. He was grateful that they'd both gotten tested and had decided to forego the condoms. It was something he'd never done with anyone else but had no doubts about being skin to skin with Mitch.

Lore pressed two lube covered fingers against Mitch's hole and laid a kiss on his shoulder blades as Mitch pushed against the intrusion, moaning as Lore's fingers slipped inside.

"That's not your cock."

Lore smiled against Mitch's neck as he pressed

his lips to the soft wet skin there. "It's coming. I don't want to hurt you."

"I'm ready. I'm more than ready. Just fuck me, Lore. *Please.*"

Lore couldn't ignore Mitch, not when he begged like that. All too aware that Mitch had been well and truly stretched this morning when they'd woken up an hour before the alarm, he quickly pulled out his fingers and lined up his cock, pausing when the head was pressing against Mitch's entrance. Lore pulled at Mitch's hips with his spare hand to manoeuvre him into a better position. "Bend over a little, babe."

Mitch shuffled his feet back and did as he was told.

"That's it. Uungh…" Lore groaned as his cock slipped passed Mitch's ring and didn't stop until it slid in to the hilt. He paused to give them both time to adjust but Mitch pulled forward causing Lore to chase him in order to keep his cock in Mitch's tight ass.

Momentum built with every thrust and it wasn't long before Mitch's moans turned into incoherent words. Lore reached around him and fisted his cock, needing Mitch to come when he did.

"I'm so close baby, come with me," Lore said against Mitch's ear. One more stroke and Mitch's cum covered the tiles in front of them. Lore released Mitch's cock as he slouched against the wall, clearly spent. Gripping onto his hips he thrust once more as Mitch's arsehole milked his cock.

They both rested like that, slumped against the wall while their bodies decided they once again belonged to them. Lore reached for the soap and quickly took care of Mitch, being nothing but gentle and loving.

After they were both clean and dry they fell into bed. Lore wasn't quite sure who'd led whom but it wasn't like that really mattered anyway. They'd laid in silence for a time just the sounds of their breaths filling the air.

Lore traced his fingers over the script tattooed on Mitch's side. "I wouldn't normally ask but it seemed kind of important. What had I walked in on earlier, at the gym?"

Mitch sighed and pressed a kiss to Lore's head. "I walked in on Wyatt and Joey discussing how they think I should get back in the ring. That it will help me."

Lore bit his lip as his fingers stopped their journey. He knew Mitch wouldn't like what he was going to say and it would probably ruin the night, but it was something Lore couldn't hold back. "I think they're right."

Mitch stiffened beneath him and Lore quickly sat up so he could see his face. "Hear me out."

Mitch breathed heavily through his nose clearly trying to tamp down his temper to do as Lore had asked.

"I don't think you should get back in the ring just for the sake of fighting, but to fight for a reason," Mitch frowned and Lore quickly carried on. "I think we should do a fundraiser for Boone's family. In his memory or honour, however you want to word it. A handful of fights, the last one being you and Wyatt. Followed by auctions of some kind. We'll get donations from local business and such."

"You've really thought this through," Mitch stated.

Lore nodded. "I have. I've been thinking about it for a while."

Mitch swallowed and turned his eyes away.

"It's okay. You don't have to do it. *We* don't have to do it. I haven't mentioned it to anyone else."

Mitch turned teary eyes on Lore. "I never thought I'd be saying this but…I want to do it. What you described makes me feel like it's right… Like I'd be doing it for a worthy reason. Yes, the fear of things going wrong is there, but taking that risk *for* Boone and his family that need to do something for them is so much greater than that fear."

Lore couldn't believe what he was hearing. He'd never even imagined telling Mitch about his idea, let alone Mitch agreeing to it. "Really?"

Mitch pulled Lore down to lie over his chest and pressed a soft kiss to his lips. "Really. How did I ever get so lucky to meet you? You know what I need when I don't even know myself."

Lore's heart skipped a beat at what he saw in Mitch's eyes. *Love.* Love that matched the love he felt for Mitch. "I want you to heal and I think this will help you do that. I just want what's best for you because I love you." The words rolled off his tongue with ease, like he'd said them a million times, when in fact this was the first time.

Mitch swallowed clearly fighting his emotions. "I love you too," he declared before taking Lore's mouth in a passion filled kiss and showing him exactly what he felt as they spent the night making love.

EPILOGUE

MITCH - EIGHTEEN MONTHS LATER

As soon as Lore had suggested raising money for Boone's wife and two kids Mitch knew it was something that he had to do. It changed his whole frame of mind. It was a way to try and make amends, even though everyone concerned had told him that he had nothing to make emends for. Even Boone's wife had told him she held nothing against Mitch when he'd met up with her to ask if she'd be happy about the event. As selfish as it may have sounded, it was a way for him to heal. And Mitch needed it more than anyone else did.

He was shaky as he stepped into the ring but he'd been training for the fight for months and it only took one swing from his opponent to have adrenaline surging through him and taking over, everything except for the ring and his opponent drifting away from him.

With each round that passed Mitch felt his punches getting stronger and his old self returning.

Wyatt was showing no signs of slowing down

and, by the time the final bell rang, the result could have gone either way. In Mitch's eyes they'd been pretty equal the whole way through.

They were pulled into the centre of the ring and the commentator spoke into the microphone. Mitch tried to work out the math in his head as the guy called out the results of each round but his heart was hammering and the blood was pumping in his ears so loudly he couldn't think straight enough to keep up.

"The winner by split decision is… the blue corner, Mitchell Sewell." The commentator's words rang in Mitch's ears and it was only his arm being thrown into the air that had him realising he'd been named the winner.

He glanced around in shock as the hall erupted into applause and cheers. Mitch's eyes landed on Lore standing in his corner, the magnificent grin spreading across his face making Mitch aware of how proud he was.

His eyes were suddenly torn away as he was pulled into a sweaty hug. "If we'd have gone twelve rounds instead of ten, I could have had you."

Mitch laughed at Wyatt's words. "You tell yourself whatever you need to get you over the loss."

They were quickly pulled apart and a microphone was shoved in front of Mitch's face. "How do you feel? There was some worry that you'd never get back in the ring again."

"I was adamant I would never get back in the ring and if Wyatt here hadn't walked into our gym all those months ago, I don't think I ever would have gotten back in." Mitch flicked his eyes to

Wyatt and gave him a smile. "So, thank you Wyatt, and thanks for the tough fight."

Mitch focused his attention back on the audience. "While I have your attention, I'd like to also thank Louisa Carter for allowing us to do this event in her husband's, Boone Carter's, memory." As his eyes roamed the crowd Louisa gave him a wide grin.

"I'd like to remind you that all the money we raise tonight will be going to his wife and children, so don't hold back when the auction starts. Lastly, I want to say a huge thank you to the man that made tonight happen, the charity event was all his idea, Lore Cole. Where are you?" The audience clapped and Mitch ran his eyes around the room looking for the man who had become his rock over the last couple of years. Mitch had seen Lore in the blue corner not five minutes earlier but now he was no longer there.

Joey stepped up, dressed in a tux, and took the microphone from the commentator. "Mr. Cole has gone to get ready for the auction, just like you should." He gave Mitch and Wyatt a pointed look. "These lovely people aren't going to want to bid for dates with smelly, sweaty men like you two."

Ah, bid for a bachelor.

That part of the auction had momentarily slipped Mitch's mind. Joey had only agreed to do it if Lore would also put himself up for grabs and Mitch hated the idea of someone else taking Lore out. He knew Lore loved him, and also knew it was more than likely to be women bidding for them all, but that didn't mean he had to like the idea of someone else getting to spend time with his man. Time Mitch felt he could be spending with Lore.

He had actually voiced that opinion more than once in the lead up to the event and all he ever got back was *"jealously isn't a good look"*, but he had a plan and Joey was right, he needed to go get ready and look his best for it.

Lore wasn't in the changing rooms when Mitch got there which was for the best because it meant he could get everything ready without the worry about being caught and having the surprise spoilt.

Once Mitch had his tux on and managed to get his bowtie just right — those things were harder to do than they looked — he pulled the little box out of his pocket and took a deep breath before opening it.

"You're really doing it."

Mitch's eyes landed on Wyatt as his stomach sank. "I should have guessed Joey wouldn't keep it to himself. Lore doesn't know, does he?"

Wyatt frowned and shook his head. "He can keep secrets from the people he needs to. Lore doesn't know a thing." Wyatt peered into the open box and Mitch admired the ring, knowing the silver band with one diamond in its centre would look perfect on Lore's finger.

As long as he said yes.

Mitch nodded.

Wyatt patted him on the back. "Well, you better hurry up and get out there before someone else snaps him up. I'm sure he's first up in the bachelor auction."

Wyatt was right. As Mitch strode back out to

the hall he could hear Joey introducing Lore on stage.

"Ladies and Gents, now I know he may look like a nerd and not much competition for the more muscular bachelors up for grabs tonight but let me assure you, Bachelor Number One has a heart of gold and I can guarantee he is the kindest guy you will ever meet."

"*Fifty dollars!*" A woman called out from the audience.

"Okay, you heard it folks, someone wants to snap him up for fifty dollars. I think he's worth more than that, what do you say?" Joey stated.

"Sixty dollars."

"Seventy."

One person after another called out and panic started to rise in Mitch's stomach. If he didn't win this bid his whole plan would fail. "Two hundred dollars," he cried out, needing the bidding to stop.

"Ladies and Gentlemen, we have a bid of two hundred dollars. Is there anyone who'd like to bid higher?"

Mitch never took his eyes off of Lore even when he stared at him in disbelief. Mitch grinned. He couldn't wait to be called the winner because that meant he could step up on that stage and —

"Going once… Going twice… Sold." Joey slammed his hand against the counter. "For two hundred dollars to the guy in the tux." He winked in Mitch's direction. "Come on up and claim your prize."

Mitch didn't need telling twice. He charged towards the stage and bounded up the few small steps until he was standing before Lore. He took in the man who meant the world to him—his dark hair styled to perfection, his tuxedo fitting like a glove, and his green eyes staring at him, looking dazed and confused.

Mitch cleared his throat as he pulled the box out of his pocket and dropped to one knee. There were gasps coming from all directions but the only one he cared about was the one that came from the man in front of him. The man he wanted to spend the rest of his life with.

Lore had covered his mouth with his hands as he looked at Mitch with wide watery eyes.

"Lorcan Cole, the day you walked into the gym was the best day of my life. I didn't know I needed you until you showed me what life was like when you had someone at your side. And I never want to be without you." Mitch swallowed the lump in his throat as he was suddenly over come by emotions. "Lore, will you spend the rest of your life with me? Will you marry me?"

Lore swallowed hard, practically mirroring Mitch only seconds ago. "Yes." He dropped to his knees and cupped Mitch's face as he peppered his lips with wet and shaky kisses. "Yes." Another kiss. "Yes. Of course I'll marry you."

Mitch pulled back before Lore could kiss him again. "Can I put the ring on now?"

"Oh, yes." Lore chuckled as he offered Mitch his hand.

Taking the ring out of the box Mitch slid it over Lore's finger and sighed in relief when it went without a fight. He'd often worried he'd spoil the moment by having bought a ring that was too small. Mitch couldn't turn his gaze away from Lore whose eyes sparkled with admiration as he took in the ring on his finger.

"I love you," Mitch announced and Lore tore his eyes from the ring, turning them onto Mitch.

Lore looked at him and, to Mitch in that moment, it felt as though Lore was staring right into his soul and seeing the truth of his words. "I love you too, Mitch. So much."

Mitch didn't know who instigated it but their lips crushed together in a passionate kiss. The room filled with applause and cheers, managing to keep them aware of the audience they had and effectively stopping them from taking things any further.

That was something Mitch would look forward to doing when they got back home. Hopefully long into the night and possibly the next day too.

"Do you realise you paid two hundred dollars to stop me from going on a date with one of my mum's book club friends?" Lore said against Mitch's cheek.

Mitch pulled back to look at Lore, who laughed the second he took in Mitch's wide eyes.

"Those bidders were your mum's friends?" Mitch asked somewhat aghast.

Lore grinned. "Yep. Mum didn't want me to look like a loser if nobody bid for me so she talked her book club friends into it." Lore's cheeks turned a bright shade of pink as he spoke.

Mitch glanced around the room looking for the woman in question whom he found standing a few feet away surrounded by a number of women and men of similar age that she was chatting to merrily. As much as Mitch wouldn't have been so upset

about Lore being on a date with a one of those people, he realised he would never have been able to
give Lore the perfect proposal if he hadn't won. It
was money well spent. He'd treasure that look that
of surprise mixed with pure bliss Lore had worn on
his face for all eternity.

Mitch hoped he'd be able to put it there again,
more than once during their marriage.

That would be his life mission.

ACKNOWLEDGEMENTS

There are so many people who support me on a daily basis and I love them all dearly for it.

First and foremost, *my family*. Thank you for keeping me grounded and not letting me lose myself in these characters and their worlds.

Kamisa Cole, you girl, go above and beyond to push me out of my comfort zone. I know you were disappointed that I waited to release this, but I couldn't bring myself to just 'throw it out there'. No matter how much faith you have in me and my words. Thank you for always believing in me. I love you tons.

To my editor, *Jane*, thank you for picking out those phrases I use that you hate. I'll never write 'in aid to' again without thinking about you.

Marisa, you really are a cover designing goddess. I love your work.

To anyone reading this, thank you for picking this book up and giving it Mitch chance. You are incredible!

Saffy XOXO

ABOUT THE AUTHOR

Saffron Blu is a romantic at heart. Spending her time writing stories where souls collide, all while looking for her own soul mate.

The mountains and beaches of SE Queensland, Australia, is where Saffron calls home. Her characters are the loudest when she's got her music blaring, drowning out the real world.

For more information:
https://saffronbluauthor.wixsite.com/books
saffronblu.author@gmail.com

Join Saffy's Facebook reader group:
https://www.facebook.com/
groups/SaffysCollidingSouls/

facebook.com/SaffronBlu

twitter.com/saffron_blu

instagram.com/saffron_blu

pinterest.com/saffron_blu

amazon.com/author/saffronblu

bookbub.com/authors/saffron-blu

goodreads.com/saffronblu

ALSO BY SAFFRON BLU

Running Hearts Series

Running Hurt - *Dom & Aimee* (MF)

Running Scared - *Matt* (Coming early 2020) (MMF)

Running Wild - *Kat* (Coming mid 2020) (FF)

Running Free - *Al* (Coming late 2020) (MM)

If you like to read MF contemporary romance, turn the page to read and excerpt of Saffron Blu's *Running Hurt*, book one of the Running Hearts Series.

The Running Hearts Series will be a four book series that follows a rock band, each book will focus on one of the band members and tell their love story.

Saffron Blu writes *stories where souls collide,* so expect to find love of all kinds in her books.

Love is Love, after all.

RUNNING HURT
ROCKSTAR LOVE IS COMPLICATED. BUT GUILTY LOVE IS IMPOSSIBLE.
RUNNING HEARTS BOOK ONE
SAFFRON BLU

CHAPTER ONE

AIMEE

I walked through the abandoned corridor feeling more and more lost as I chatted to my best friend on the phone. "Sammy, I'm telling you I'm fucking lost. I can't tell you where I am other than a nondescript abandoned corridor."

"Okay, stop and breathe. We'll figure this out. The band aren't going to be on stage for another twenty minutes, we have plenty of time to find you." Sam let out an excited breath. "Oh, I've got an idea, hang on."

The sound of rustling came through the line, and I pulled the phone away from my ear to glare at it. I glanced around the corridor and decided to keep walking. It had to end somewhere, right?

Voices were getting louder, and relief ran through me knowing someone was nearby. Maybe they'd be able to direct me back to the stands.

Suddenly, something hit me hard, sending a shooting pain down the left side of my body. I dropped to the floor in a pain filled heap.

"Fuck." The word sounded distant as blackness engulfed me.

My eyes flicked open and I saw a blurry face looking down at me. Blinking rapidly, my eyes started to clear and a familiar set of mismatched eyes looked back at me with concern.

"I'm hallucinating…I'm fucked."

That was what it had to be; there was no way Dominic Saxton was crouched beside me on the floor encouraging me back to consciousness. Yes, he may have been in the building but he wasn't going to be walking around and at risk of being hounded by overzealous fans. Wanting to shake this stupid hallucination away I tried to think of what I was doing before it started; *talking to Sam.*

"Sam," I said, pushing to sit up. Moving made my head spin and my stomach churn so I quickly decided lying on the floor was the better option.

A very male chuckle close by had my eyes popping open. Was it still a hallucination if it was just sound?

"I don't go by Sam. And last I checked I wasn't a hallucination." He pulled the same smirk I'd seen a thousand times in his interviews. "I'm Dom," he added.

Dominic Saxton was a singer songwriter whose artist name was just Saxton. His band—Running Hearts—was made up of him, his sister and best friend. Their debut song hit number one worldwide and stayed there for weeks; which was why they were currently doing a sellout world tour.

Sam and I had travelled to America especially to see the concert at the last stop, believing the last was always the best show. We figured it was a great way to get us to travel the world a little, which was something we'd discussed numerous times. I had three kids and, having just come out of a messy divorce, it was good to be able to have some 'me time' while the kids were spending the school holidays with their dad—my douche canoe of an ex-husband.

I'd left Sam in the cafeteria while I followed signs for the bathrooms only to go off track and find myself wandering abandoned corridors.

My hand lifted of its own accord and I poked a finger at his chest, before snatching my hand back. "Huh… you *do* feel real."

Jesus! The knock to my head must've done more damage than I thought. I wished it *were* all a hallucination now.

I tried to sit up again, moving slower than before but Dom pressed his palms against my shoulders effectively holding me to the floor.

"You have some wicked bruises, it's probably best if you don't move. Not until the paramedics check you out anyway." He winced as he looked at my face and I hoped to hell it was just a bruise he was wincing at and not my natural look.

I could hear fast footsteps approaching.

"This is all they had in the freezer." The voice was female and I couldn't help but wonder who it might be. Being jealous was pointless. He was a rockstar, he probably had a busload of female groupies following him around and doing anything he wanted.

I watched Dom smile at the new arrival and take something off her. "Thanks, Sis."

My jealousy was washed away with that one word.

Sis.

That was right, the band was made up of family —his sister playing the drums alongside him. The media had made a big deal about their brother also being with them for the tour, but he was yet to actually be seen on stage so I had no idea what he'd been doing—and the media didn't seem to know either.

Dom turned his attention back to me. "I've got some ice here that I'm going to press to your cheek. I'll be gentle, I promise."

He didn't wait for me to reply, just reached out and placed the cold hard pack against the side of my face. I hissed but he didn't relent.

"Matt has gone to get your friend, Sam," Dom explained. "She was still on the cell when you blacked out."

The thought that he might have been trying to distract me from the pain ran through my mind before his sister spoke up. "She was crying bloody murder down the line until one of us told her what was happening."

Dom's eyes were on his sister and I grabbed his arm to get his attention. When his eyes locked on mine I gave him a demanding stare. "She knows I'm okay though, right?"

He swallowed nervously. "Well, you were still out of it when Matt left to find her."

Letting go of his arm I reached around the floor feeling for my phone. Sam was a born worrier which meant she'd be freaking the hell out. "My phone? We need to call her."

His warm hand engulfed my searching one, instantly stilling it. "Matt took it. It'll probably be easier finding her if they keep talking."

I sighed and relaxed on the floor, knowing the only person who could distract her from freaking would have been Matthew Dalcin, Dom's best mate and guitarist. Maybe I should've thanked my lucky stars that it was those three that had knocked me out with the door and not just a random stranger. "Who knocked me out with the door?" I asked. The small frown I attempted caused my face to throb.

Dom weighed me up before grinning. "That depends…are you thinking of suing? Because if so, it was Matt."

I laughed. "Well, since you're a shit liar, I guess it's a good job I'm not the suing type."

He let out his own hearty laugh before fresh voices approached.

"Holy fuck! Aimee, are you alright?" Sam's calm tone relaxed me in an instant. There may have been worry behind her words, but not a complete freak out so that was good.

"I'm okay as long as I don't move."

Sam crouched down beside me, making Dom move away and stand beside his sister.

"Jesus, Aims, your face is a mess." Sam glared at Dom, and I took a moment to close my eyes. As adrenaline began to leave my body, pain seemed to take over.

"Aims?" Sam's worried tone whispered beside me.

"I feel like I've been hit by a truck." I breathed as shallowly as I could, trying not to move.

More voices caught my attention but I didn't open my eyes. If I did, tears would've fallen and I didn't want to look like a wimp in front of my celebrity crush.

"She's just up here," a new male voice announced.

Two paramedics crouched down beside me, gently pressing at my face. After a few minutes of assessing the rest of my body, the older of the two got up and stepped away.

"Aimee, do you think you'd be able to get up and make it to the stretcher?" the younger paramedic asked.

Taking a moment to assess my body and its relevant aches and pains, I decided the only way I would really know was to try. "I guess I could try."

Very slowly, I moved to an upright position. It hurt, but I could handle it.

The younger paramedic took my left arm and Dom appeared at my right, a hand under my elbow ready to catch me if I fell. I stopped holding my breath once I was laid back on the stretcher and gave Dom a grateful smile for his helping hand. "Thanks."

"Don't thank me. I'm the idiot who opened the door into your face. I'm so sorry about that by the way." He shook his head, wincing again as he looked at my face.

"Do I look that bad?"

"You look awful, Aims," Sam said, stopping at my other side on the stretcher.

"Who is coming with us? There's only room for one," the older paramedic asked.

"That'll be me," Sam stated.

"You will not. If I have to miss the concert, you better take a million photos and record all my favorite songs." The panic was audible in my voice.

We had paid so much to be there and there was no way I was letting Sam miss it.

No fucking way!

Sam looked at me, indecision clear on her face.

"I'll go with her," offered the guy who'd brought the paramedics in. He stared at Dom. "I know you'll want to be kept in the loop since you'll be paying her medical expenses."

"I…no, I can pay them myself!" I protested. I'd already told them I wasn't the suing type. I didn't expect him to pay my bills just because he'd opened a door that I happened to be on the other side of.

Dom brushed a strand of hair off my face. The gesture seemed too intimate for someone who'd only just met me but, nevertheless, I liked it. "I caused this. At least let me pay to fix it."

The pleading look he had plastered over his face had me nodding before I'd even thought about it.

"Great. So it's sorted. Sam's going to record your favorite songs for you and my brother, Alberto, is going to accompany you to the hospital. He'll give them my details so they can send me the bill." He looked at his brother, who nodded, and then turned his attention to Sam.

She huffed, but I could see the defeat in her slouched shoulders. She was going to fold. "Fine." Her stern look left Dom and softened as her eyes fell on me. "So, that means you want every song recorded since they're all your favorites."

"Yep, but you love me too much not to do it."

She rolled her eyes. "Ugh, you're right." Turning to Alberto she placed my phone in his hand. "It's Aimee's cell, I'm Sam. You text me the minute the doctors tell you anything." Her tone was insistent and although she hadn't added a threat, I knew one was hiding there somewhere.

He dipped his head. "Sure thing."

The paramedics started to wheel me down the corridor and Alberto kept pace along side us. "She's quite scary, your friend."

The genuine unsettled tone in his voice made me laugh. "Yeah, she can be sometimes."

It didn't take them long to get us loaded into the ambulance and on our way to the hospital. Alberto chatted away to me about all kinds of mundane crap. I think he was just trying to distract me from the pain but the paramedics had given me a green whistle to suck on, which was fabulous. After about five minutes I started to feel lightheaded. I assumed it was the drugs so when the machine beside me started beeping chaotically and the older paramedic's voice started to sound anxious I didn't worry — or maybe that was the drugs too.

I didn't really care, I'd just met my celebrity crush and I was on cloud nine because of it.